FLAGSHIP

A. J. Converse

1

A.J. Converse

DEDICATION

This novel is dedicated to the men who served aboard the
USS *Eldorado* AGC-11 through all her years

*"I can imagine no more rewarding a career. And any man who may be
asked in this century what he did to make his life worthwhile, I think can respond
with a good deal of pride and satisfaction: "I served in the United States Navy."*

~John F. Kennedy
1963

FICTION

This novel is fiction. Any resemblance of characters to real
people is coincidental.

PROLOGUE

January 1943

John Mayer examined his weld. It ran sturdy and straight, only rising out of true toward the port end of the deck plate. Off center and slightly higher than the line, it maintained the integrity of the connection between plates but lost something in aesthetics. Mayer, a perfectionist, muttered under his breath.

"Sum bitch, too late to redo it."

The foreman pushed hard today. As long as the structure stayed sound he would clear it. Mayer hated rushed work. If he could he would re-weld the entire section, but war put a rush on every ship. No screwing around with aesthetics.

The liberty ships went out of the yard, one every few days. This vessel was different, a C-2 hull, quality mattered, but not perfection.

3

War stormed through the world, like the late-January blustery gusts blowing up the seaway from the Cape Fear River to the great ship's growing hull, the blasts unstoppable, like Nazi Blitzkrieg attacks. His mind shifted to Helen and the little one. Tiny Earnest Royal, the middle name after his great-grandfather, two months old, waited at home with his mother. The world war growled ugly, ready to engulf them. Mayer stood between his wife and kid and the poor house. The job did anyway. Mayer's shipyard work kept the draft away from him and paid a decent wage. Still, his country beckoned.

The foreman yelled, "Knock-off, knock-off, second shift arriving. Wrap it up."

Mayer pushed up his welding helmet, felt the cold wind against his perspiration soaked face.

"Hey, boss, take a look at this."

"Good 'nuff for government work. Wrap it up."

"What da ya mean government work?"

"The Navy wants it."

"Ya know what happened to those Liberty ships, broke up . . . bad welds." Mayer persisted.

The foreman examined the twenty-six-year-old welder, lean, brawny from manual labor. Mayer, his blond hair wet with sweat, stared back with hard blue eyes.

He spoke, his voice raspy. "This weld's okay, just ugly. Come on wrap it up, I wanna go home."

~

Mayer stowed his welding gear and headed down the gangplank to the dry dock. Images of war, the Nazis, the Japs, spun in his mind.

What good is a house if the Germans reach the US and burn it down, or the Japanese?

They wanted to purchase the house they rented on Port Street, not far from the shipyard. Home ownership would have to wait if he enlisted. Helen would be proud, but scared for him. She and Earnest would move in with her folks for the war's duration.

I have to go. The future, everything, depends on us winning.

He shook his head. Plans change, he learned that when little Ernie came, a surprise. The elderly lady who owned the house offered to sell it to them once they saved a thousand dollars for the down payment and if they found a bank to carry a four-thousand-dollar mortgage. Mayer's shipyard job promised the house. They could swing it in a couple of years.

In Casablanca, the Allies had agreed to demand unconditional surrender from the Axis powers. Mayer realized a massive influx of troops from America would be needed to liberate Europe and bring Germany to its knees. The Japanese showed no sign of weakness. They held the Philippines and many islands in the South Pacific.

Perhaps this ship, the *Monsoon,* to be launched later in the year, and eventually to be delivered to the Navy, would help. In any event he had to join the fight. He decided to enlist.

~

June 6, 1944

John Mayer huddled low in his Higgins boat with thirty-five fellow soldiers. His platoon, part of the 116th Regiment, pulled from the 129th Division, to expand the Army's 1st Division, landing first wave. Their job: to support the elite Rangers assigned to hit the cliffs of Omaha Beach. He

5

didn't care for all the rah-rah stuff about regimental honor. He worried about dying.

The thunder of naval gunfire from all the guns in the world, it seemed, echoed in his ears. He fingered the rosary in his pocket, a gift from his mom, and recited the Hail Mary in a continuous mantra of fear. He peeked upward to see the sky, bleak and overcast with drizzle and the promise of death everywhere. If he survived to reach the landing zone he intended to hit it face down at a squirm. The hell with a heads up charge, when the bow door dropped he was going in low, hoping to avoid the German bullets from the machine guns and carbines packing the high points of the beach.

"Oh, God," he prayed, "get me through this."

A jolt hammered the bottom, followed by a scream from the coxswain, "We're going down. We hit a barrier. Bow door down, bow door down, jump in the water. Ya gotta wade."

A sailor not the platoon leader, he couldn't order Army guys.

Sarge bellowed, "Ya wanna live forever, come on."

The door was down, the water flowed in cold, numbing. Mayer joined the others, flailing out the bow as the deck submerged. Shoulders and heads bobbed and disappeared under the rushing seawater.

"Too deep, too deep," someone screamed.

He stumbled, pushed by desperate hands behind him. With water sloshing on his chest, and praying the Hail Mary, he stepped off the boat into hell. The cold ocean closed in upon him. No chance to squirm on the beach and avoid German machine guns, Mayer sunk to the bottom before he could slip out of his back pack. He dropped his gun somewhere.

Who cares? Swim. Fight to the surface.

He wiggled out of the pack, pushed up on numbing legs, thrashing his arms, forgetting all he knew about swimming. A boot from above shoved him down, some desperate brother in a panic. He swallowed water, thrashed some more, and hit the surface gasping. Others struggled around him.

The beach glowed red, orange, white hot as heavy artillery rounds from the offshore guns blasted at the German lines. Plinks and splashes hit everywhere in the water from shrapnel and machine-gun bullets. The shots not splashing killed.

"Hail Mary, full of grace." Mayer repeated the mantra as he floundered, found some footing, waded. No charging the beach while firing his gun like in all the training, no squirming through the foam, just flailing trying to stay alive, no pack, no gun.

Stay down, squirm.

Like a different person, he was out of his body floating above and screaming.

Stay down crawl, stay alive.

Mayer crawled past bloody bodies toward a high point. *Cover!* Something scraped at him. A GI, eyes pleading, scratched with the stub of a forearm, his other arm completely gone. *No hope for him.* Mayer shook him off. Desperation drove him. Somewhere he lost a boot. He reached the tiny oasis in the torrent of lead screaming past him. He huddled there.

A peek to the rear told him everything. Bodies and crying, wounded GIs everywhere. We won't hold, he thought. He huddled in the sand hoping friendly Germans would capture him after the fight. The shore fire from the sea intensified. He looked around again; saw another wave of Higgins boats headed toward him. *Poor bastards.*

7

He passed out or slept, he didn't know. He woke as a GI poked him.

"What unit soldier?" the sergeant shouted above the din.

"Third platoon, 116th," he said.

"First wave, eh? Look, grab an M-1 off one of the dead guys, find a shoe that fits ya and join my group over there." He pointed twenty yards away to a pit carved out by some ship's errant shell.

Mayer scuttled over to a body, picked up the gun and some ammo, grabbed the left shoe and scrambled over to the other men. He was in the fight again. Eleven GIs hunched down in the shell hole, one with an obvious wound to his arm, the others with mental wounds which would never heal.

"Look, I'm here to fight Germans. My platoon was supposed to take a positon up the beach there." The sergeant pointed at a pillbox spitting out sporadic fire.

"Two of us made it here . . . the rest are dead." He was screaming now. "You guys are from other platoons. You can stay here and cower, but I think our only chance is to knock out that pillbox and secure the high ground."

"How long you been in this war, Sarge," one shouted.

"Two years."

"That's about eighteen months more than me. Okay I'm with ya."

"Name's Weinstein, by-the-way," Sarge said.

The older man by a few years, Mayer doubted the plan's wisdom, but there didn't seem to be any other options.

"Okay, follow me guys," Weinstein bellowed and started crawling up the beach. Mayer followed and soon found himself next to the sargent

Sell your books at sellbackyourBook.com!

Go to sellbackyourBook.com and get an instant price quote. We even pay the shipping - see what your old books are worth today!

Inspected By:eva_toledano

00031544568

on a slight rise twenty yards from the pillbox. Weinstein handed him a grenade and fingered one himself.

"Guys, open up on the pillbox," he shouted." We'll run up and dump our grenades inside."

They started shooting.

Sarge jumped up. Mayer followed.

~

As retired Sergeant Major Weinstein told his grandkids years later, "I looked over at the man from the 116th when a bunch of machine gun bullets hit his face. They took the head clean off except for the sides. Two ears hung in the air by themselves. He was gone just like that."

Mayer fell. His body rolled a few feet into a shell hole.

The next day a tank rigged with a dozer blade plowed a path for other vehicles over the shell hole. Private John Mayer, welder of deck plates for the *SS Monsoon*, which the Navy christened *USS Eldorado*, died one cold June day on the beaches of France, and became a "missing in action."

~

Helen learned first and thanked God little Ernie wouldn't understand. To him the world included his mother and a vague other person. The telegram said "missing in action," the most terrible thing. Missing probably meant dead, but presented a slim hope, diabolical in nature, a hope that would dig at Helen's heart for years after Ernie grew to maturity.

9

1

January 1967

The young man from Alabama first came to his attention at sea on the way to WESTPAC. Bode, one of Winthrop's third-class boatswain's mates, stood watching half-a-dozen sailors in work denims chipping paint on the forward boat deck. They used hand chisels and hammers. The ship stocked power chippers and power drills rigged with wire brushes, but the sailors worked the old way. Orders from Nobel, he figured as he walked toward the group. His stride adjusted to the ship's roll and pitch as *Eldorado* took the sets off the starboard bow. The great Pacific Ocean surrounded the aging flagship, a relative speck amidst the hard blue waves and cold white froth on the brisk winter day.

The sailors engaged in a routine chore at sea, assigned as much to keep them busy as to maintain the steel deck. The ship plowed ahead at a steady twelve knots, a long way to WESTPAC and a long way from Hawaii, their last port of call.

Zachary Lee sang some sort of ditty as he chipped away.

> *Roll me over in the clover, roll me over lay me down and do it again;*
> *This is number three and my hand is on her knee;*
> *Roll me over in the clover, roll me over lay me down and do it again;*
> *This is number four, threw her on the floor;*
> *Roll me over in the clover, roll me over lay me down and do it again*

Flagship

A new man, not yet a seaman, and assigned randomly to first division, Lee had reported aboard a month or so before, a few days before *Eldorado's* deployment, fresh out of boot camp, eager for sea duty, the quintessential sailor.

"Morning sir," Bode said and grinned. "Turning to?"

Lieutenant junior grade Winthrop wiggled two fingers. "How's it going Bode? Who's the vocalist?"

"Lee, he can sing, I guess, twenty-three or more verses of the song."

The other sailor's, all white guys, egged on the singer. Bode waved his hand at the black sailor and shrugged.

Lee was trying to make friends.

"When's he go on the watch list?" Winthrop said.

"Soon, I think, but Nobel wants him to learn the messenger-of-the-watch duties first."

"Looks like you're nearly done here."

"Ya, but I gotta keep a couple sailors to cover the bare steel with red lead."

"Stop by the deck office and see me before lunch. Tell Nobel I want to see him before lunch too."

"Aye sir."

In the combat zone, high activity under tense conditions would leave little time for personnel. Now while in transit he wanted to be certain his division was squared away. Zachary Lee promised to be a good sailor if he handled things right. Ha, "squared away," he thought, "navy talk," was he becoming an old salt?

What am I doing here?

11

His mind jumped back to a rooftop on Commonwealth Avenue. So many times he thought of that blonde girl. *What was her name?* He could never remember, she merged with that idyllic summer. The summer he decided to stay in Boston, working part-time before his junior year, before he decided the Navy's reserve officer program offered his best bet to handle the draft.

Her eager sex, and the liquor, and Boston in the summer all merged in his mind to embody a time without obligations, without cares. Since he joined the reserves, his thinking evolved from party, party, enjoy the party, to a more serious question what to do with his life. The weekly reserve meetings suggested what the Navy offered for three years after college but didn't answer the big question. *What do I do with my life?*

Winthrop continued his rounds, checking the guy wires on the ship's boats, admired the admiral's barge, stored on racks, forward of the bridge, his responsibility. He moved past the five-inch gun next and checked the pelican hooks on the anchor chains, all routine walk-around-look-see work for a junior officer in the deck division. He lit a cigarette, drew a puff and tossed it over the side. Gotta quit he thought.

2

Winthrop pulled out his gray steel chair, sat at a Navy standard gray desk, and nodded at Lieutenant Joe Trucker, deck department head, who sat in a similar desk outboard of Winthrop. Trucker, wearing brown uniform boots now hooked back under his chair, surrounded by status boards and files, the paraphernalia of administration for the hundred or so sailors and three officers of the deck department, grunted greetings and bent over his work. Gage, the department yeoman, sat typing across the small space of the long, narrow office.

Winthrop threw his hat on the desk, settling in. He supervised around fifty of those men, all part of first division.

Bode stopped by first, doffed his white hat. Sincere, respectful, the nineteen-year-old, stood short at five feet, six or so, but sturdy, sporting a Navy buzz cut on the sides and bushy hair on top.

"Wanted to see me, sir?"

"I wanna show you something," Fred said and turned to Trucker.

"Be back in a few minutes," he said.

He led Bode through the passage past the ship's store and up a ladder through a hatch to the main deck.

"Hey, I'm gonna assign Lee as starboard lookout on my watch rotation."

"Don't know if he's ready."

Winthrop raised his voice. "He will be if you stop the lollygagging with your sailors. You're a new petty officer, what's more important for sailors aboard ship being liked or respected?"

Winthrop didn't let him answer, moved close.

13

"I'll tell ya, respect. Never join the men under your supervision in patronizing another sailor. When we're in the combat zone, you'll need respect and Lee'll need it too."

Winthrop swallowed his trepidation at disciplining a man only a few years younger and went on.

"Right now those men think you're their buddy and Lee thinks he's gotta entertain to be part of the crew. Next time he starts singing stop him, say something like 'knock it off, this is a US Navy ship,' or anything. Just stop him."

Winthrop calmed his still loud voice.

"The guys'll be perturbed, but they'll respect you and Lee will have a better chance to be a good sailor."

"I'm being chewed out."

"Yeah." Winthrop lowered his voice to normal, "Now look, we gotta go over your section personnel. I wanna update my training records."

Winthrop led him back to the deck office.

Nobel entered as Bode was leaving.

"I checked out the red lead earlier, Bode," Winthrop said, to the petty officer, now heading for the door. "A good job, when do ya think you can get it painted?"

"Huh, oh, tomorrow if we don't hit a squall." Bode glanced at Nobel.

"You wanted to see me, sir?" Nobel said and pulled up a chair, turned it to sit backwards.

Nobel's face sported more scars than a prizefighter. Busted a couple of times, he always came back. Now off booze and shooting for the CPO mess, he had taken the test for chief. Fred hoped to hear on the promotion by the time *Eldorado* got to Subic Bay. Soft spoken for a first class boatswain's mate but as physical and tough minded as they came, his reputation told of winning many a brawl in bars around the world.

"Got this opening for assault boat coxswain school," Winthrop said. "Gage says he'd like to attend. We'll need to find another yeoman for the department."

Seaman Mark Gage turned in his chair. "It's the school I was askin' about, Nobel."

"No objection," Nobel said. "You get that designation and you might find yourself driving a platoon load of Marines in a LCVP up on the beach under enemy fire."

"I'm okay with that," and he handed an already complete request to Winthrop for his signature. After Nobel initialed it, Winthrop signed.

"I wanna put Lee on my watch rotation as starboard lookout." Winthrop lit another cigarette. The watch protocol switched the lookout every hour on each four hour watch. Thus the starboard lookout rotated to the aft station, the port station, and back to starboard on each watch. The system helped keep them alert.

"Aye sir. Johnson wanted him to learn messenger-of-the-watch first."

"Johnson can start walking him through the ropes as messenger, no harm in him starting as a lookout at the same time. No extra training needed. He learned that lookout stuff in boot camp."

Winthrop leaned back in his gray steel chair; put his foot on an open drawer.

"Say about Johnson, make sure he doesn't pass off Lee's training to anyone else. Lee needs a little something, Aww . . ."

"The black thing?"

15

Johnson, a black man with an edge, but a competent second class petty officer, would stop Lee from playing the clown for his white shipmates.

"Ya noticed?"

"Ya," Nobel said. "Anyway I want to pull Hampton off the port lookout on your watch. I want to teach that sailor about respect for a first class. Maybe assign him to latrine duty for a while. Why not put Lee on the port side instead?"

"The soon-to-be-chief feeling his oats, huh? Sounds good. Okay we'll do that." Winthrop checked his watch. "Eleven-thirty, time to hit the wardroom."

Nobel pointed at Winthrop's belt and grinned. "Hey, boss, you're getting to be an old salt. You're wearing a deck knife."

Winthrop rubbed a tarnished silver bar on the collar of his wash khaki work uniform. "Always liked deck better than operations," he said. "It's the real Navy."

After Officer Candidate School, Uncle Sam assigned Winthrop to the position of OA division officer, part of the operations department, after some extra schooling. The division supplied aerographer, print, photo, and drafting services for the admiral's staff when embarked, and for surrounding ships when the commander, amphibious forces pacific fleet moved to one of *Eldorado's* two sister ships.

Eldorado would host the admiral and his staff of fifty or so officers and men once they arrived in Subic Bay. A heavy schedule of operations in the combat zone would ensue.

Winthrop relished his current duties in deck coupled with his bridge watch duties. A precursor to his current job involved establishing the trust of the captain and the various department heads. Winthrop's diligent attention to his duty got around the ship. People talk, and with over 500 men crammed on a ship 459 feet long and 60 feet wide, everyone soon knows a man's personal standards and competency. He didn't understand his own strong commitment. He was a ninety-day wonder with no hope to compete with Annapolis graduates for higher levels in a Navy career. He planned only to serve out his three-year active duty obligation. Had Vietnam not exploded he'd be working in some bank somewhere. *So Why?*

He savored first division's vital role in the deployment. From anchoring to loading supplies and refueling at sea as well as operating the ship's officer's boats, his department was the real Navy.

In his first assignment with OA division the print jobs, photo shoots, and drafting jobs of his old division, primarily useful for public affairs, only rarely handled sensitive or vital subjects. They could as well have been civilian jobs. The modern Navy got plenty of weather information so the weather shop of OA division existed as an Admiral's perk.

Joe Trucker grunted from his chair. "Come on, Salty, let's get some chow."

~

Nobel

Bode got his ass chewed. I'm sure. He could read the signs. That red lead comment of Winthrop's told Bode he wouldn't share whatever Bode screwed up with the first class. Years in the Navy taught Nobel how to read men.

The effect of Nobel's upbringing in Maine, like his down Maine accent affected his speech sometimes, left minor remnants in his

17

personality. Sometimes he dreamed of retiring and getting a cabin in the woods. When his memories of fishing for brookies in the cold water streams and hunting deer in the fall woods touched his consciousness like wisps of an alternate universe he recognized them to be fantasies. *You can't go back. Someone said that.*

Nobel figured Winthrop was a pretty good officer as JGs go. Nobel could count on him. He wasn't lazy or arrogant like some he met in his career. And he wasn't blindly officious when common sense offered a non-Navy solution to a problem. *But did he have the juice to propel Nobel into the CPO mess?*

~

Trucker sat at the wardroom head table with the XO and the other department heads as Winthrop took his place at one of the junior officer tables.

He snuffed out his cigarette on the table ashtray, pulled his linen napkin out of his personalized ring, used as a place setting.

Lieutenant junior grade Tom Randolph, second division officer, who supervised another forty of deck department's sailors, and a talker but a hell of a good buddy on the beach, blustered on about poisonous sea snakes in the South China Sea.

"Two steppers, I tell ya." He said to the new guy, Ensign Harley Larsen, fresh out of OCS via Colorado State where he majored in marketing.

Larsen, not yet assigned a division, was learning the ship. Part of the operations division, he would likely take over OA division once he got oriented. Now he stood training watches and wrote reports for the operations officer, a lieutenant commander, third in command succession,

18

head of the operations department, and senior watch officer. Winthrop knew the drill.

"Ya think a rattler is scary," Randolph said, "wait till you see one of these bastards."

Chief warrant officer "Chips" Beasley, the ship's carpenter, listened while pulling on his unlit corn-cob pipe. A little man, bald, with years of sea duty, he adjusted his spectacles and waited for the stewards to finish serving the table, placed his pipe on the white linen tablecloth and offered some advice.

"You two won't know what a poisonous snake is," he said, "until ya run into a snow snake."

Randolph stopped dead in his bluster. "Huh?" His chubby face, topped with black hair offset with perpetual rosy cheeks, Indian blood, Winthrop figured, flushed.

Chips sprang his trap. "Aye-ya, in way northern Vermont they got this snake, pure white, don't ya know." He lapsed into a deep New England accent. "The little bugger crawls up yer ass and freezes ya to death."

Winthrop passed some milk through his nose.

When the laughter eased to chuckles, Chips said, "I'm waitin' to see what happens when young mister Larsen gets turned loose on the bars and brothels of Southeast Asia. Hope they are ready."

Winthrop knew that drill too.

Beasley turned to Winthrop. "Ya got the twelve to four Fred?"

Winthrop nodded.

"Nothing going on," Chips said, "but the chief engineer will want us to blow tubes during your watch. Give you something to do. You can designate Mister Larsen to do it, train him you know."

19

Larsen, standing taller than Winthrop, but boney, with dark blond hair and slate grey eyes exuded the kind of confidence Winthrop recalled seeing in other recent OCS graduates. Larsen fathomed far less than he thought he knew.

"Big deal," Larsen said.

Winthrop finished eating, replaced the personalized ring on his napkin, and nodded at Larsen. "We better get up there."

3

Lieutenant Steve Taylor bent over the deck log, signing out. Taylor at six feet, stood about the same height as Winthrop. Taylor lighter-skinned of the two, with blond hair, Winthrop, more muscled, trim, they faced each other, saluted, and Winthrop said, "I assume the watch."

He turned to face the rest of the wheelhouse gang and spoke in a loud voice, "This is Mister Winthrop. I have the *conn*."

The "Aye, aye, sir's" came back from the bridge crew.

Only the Captain superseded the officer of the deck, who generally took the *conn*, a mantle held by only one man on a ship. The OOD could assign the mantle to the junior officer of the deck only, but remained responsible for anything the JOOD did. One man alone on the vessel could take the conn without the OOD's say so, the captain. The executive officer, a full commander, could not order the OOD, only the captain. On watch, the OOD commanded instant obedience from all hands because, second to the captain, he alone stood responsible for the safety of the crew. As a result, the qualification as OOD, underway steaming, was not issued without due consideration. Many junior naval officers never received the designation. A jet pilot qualified to land on a carrier performed a more dangerous duty, but remained responsible only for himself and his plane.

Winthrop's senses peaked on the bridge. He understood the responsibility. Approximately 450 men went about their duties dependent on his judgement to keep the vessel, their home and workplace, a tiny speck in the middle of the ocean, safe.

The helmsman, the engine order phone talker, the bridge phone talker, the look outs, after steering, the quartermaster of the watch, the boatswain's mate of the watch all came under his direct control.

In the engine room two fire men stood by the two boilers. Each boiler could handle three burners which burned fuel oil sprayed on the tubes which in turn heated the steam for the turbines. Two burners kept the ship at cruising speed of 12 knots. An extra burner had to be added if the officer of the deck called for flank speed. The engine room gang huddled under an air blower that kept the heat in the cavernous room tolerable. A top man stood above watching pressure indicators and a similar bottom man watched other pressure indicators.

In the combat information center radarmen under the OOD's control searched the sky and surface miles out from the ship for contacts.

As Winthrop toured his bridge, checking his crew, Harley Larsen relieved another new ensign who was learning the elements of ship-handling as junior officer of the deck. The young officer waved Larsen over to the radar repeater on the starboard side.

Winthrop didn't appreciate having to train Harley Larsen, too new and to cocky in his opinion, to try out on bridge watches. But arguing with the senior watch officer proved pointless.

Larsen walked over to him.

"Fred," Larsen said, passing on the radar information, "we got a contact about fifteen miles out, off the starboard bow, closest point of approach, across the bow at ten miles."

"Good, go ahead and take the conn. We got a course change coming up at 1500. You'll be able to handle that."

The navigator had laid out a great circle route for *Eldorado* to save time in the long passage. Winthrop examined the chart, a featureless sheet of paper except for the penciled in latitude and longitude lines. A series of three pointed fixes adorned the sheet running up the center, near the route already laid out, Eldorado's track. The fixes came from stars at night and sun lines in the day if the weather was clear. The bearing lines rarely intersected in a perfect point, thus the fixes amounted to an eyeball judgment point placed in the center of the triangle. LORAN bearing lines from special radio signals beamed by Navy beacons produced tighter fixes, but the navigators on Navy ships used celestial bodies as much as possible in order to maintain the skill. The route required a course change of a couple of degrees every few hours.

Winthrop walked across the swaying gray steel deck to the port lookout station. Cerulean blue skies littered with clumps of cumulus clouds turned the sea hard blue, a typical mid-pacific ocean day. The water-covered earth in this remote spot offered neither solace nor eminent danger to humans venturing on the water in steel ships. The sailors themselves determined how events affected them. The sea remained a silent observer, neither helpful nor menacing, just water, cold, unaffected.

Boatswain Mate Second Class Johnson stood talking with Lee, and fingering his boatswain's pipe. The formal, lanky, and dark-brown sailor said, "Afternoon sir," and stared through lidded eyes revealing nothing but expressing a distain that disturbed Winthrop.

"Afternoon," Winthrop kept his own voice and countenance blank.

"How ya doin'," he said to Lee, putting friendliness into his voice. "Keep your eyes peeled over toward starboard." And he pointed off the starboard bow, a bit away from the port lookout sector. "See if you can spot our contact before the starboard lookout does."

"Aye, aye, sir." Lee's eyes lit up.

23

Johnson, ignoring Winthrop, walked over to the chronometer, checked it, moved to the 1 MC, blew his pipe and announced. "Now secure the mess deck."

~

Johnson

Another white boy officer.

Johnson didn't trust any of the officers. He never met a black officer. He doubted the Navy allowed them. Winthrop tried to take off his brass hat with Johnson sometimes but Johnson never relaxed with him. It pissed him off that Winthrop always assigned black sailors to him to train. Why not white guys? I treat them all the same. Winthrop and Nobel joked around sometimes, Johnson would never do that.

Don't let your guard down. They'll screw you every time.

With rigor, Johnson followed his script for the watch. He figured if he messed up the routine of 1MC announcements, Winthrop or some other white officer would use it against him, try to get a white boy boatswain's mate on the bridge to replace him.

The bridge, out on the Pacific, Johnson liked daylight duty up there. The brightness streamed in the ports on the wheelhouse and through its two hatches, port and starboard, leading out to the wings where the lookouts stood scanning for threats which never seemed to arise. Only the great wooden wheel, the sturdy wood platform for the helmsman and the white paper spread over the quartermaster's chart table broke the haze grey color of the bulkheads and darker grey on the deck. Of course the brass of the voice tubes, located strategically as last ditch communication devices and the brass on the compass binnacle in front of the helm stood out. The bridge brass, shined daily by sailors from the navigation division, never saw a bit of tarnish.

24

Flagship

Sailors in work dungarees and white hats bustled performing various watch standing tasks. Johnson knew his job, pipe the daily routine, pipe emergency orders to the crew, and maintain order and discipline on the bridge for the OOD. In a few minutes he would inform Winthrop he was heading aft to check on the after lookout.

~

Twelve-thirty, this watch is moving fast, Winthrop thought. He wandered into the wheelhouse again thinking of running an after-steering drill to wake-up those guys back aft, deep in the hull, down by the manual rudder control, a wheel attached through some gears which controlled the immense rudder in an emergency. Strong sailors were needed on that station because there was no hydraulic assist.

The quartermaster of the watch bent over the chart table marking the latest fix on the chart. He looked up and whispered to Winthrop, "Captain's on the bridge sir."

"Thanks." He looked back to the port wing and said "Afternoon Captain."

"Afternoon, Fred," Ridgway said. "Carry on. I'm just getting a little fresh air." He pulled down his gold brimmed hat and walked over to a padded raised chair identical to another attached to the deck on the starboard wing of the bridge. Rue the officer or enlisted man who ever presumed to sit on the captain's chair at any time.

The 21 MC squawked. "Bridge, engine room, request permission to blow tubes."

Ensign Larsen headed over to the intercom.

Winthrop reached out and grabbed his arm. "Wait a minute. What're you gonna say?"

"Permission granted. What's the big deal?"

25

"Goddamn it. Check the relative wind first. Ya wanna blow soot all over the captain there?"

Larsen, taller than Winthrop, cocked his head back, turned his lanky frame and checked the wind indicator. "Almost no relative wind."

"That's because we got a tail wind. Don't ever think any action on the bridge is routine. Always think and double check. If you gave them permission just now, you would have the whole ship mad at me. The deck crew would have to swab all the decks. They did that this morning. The captain would chew my ass up one side and down the other; maybe kick me off the bridge."

Winthrop dropped his voice. "Okay now what you gonna do?"

"I guess I'll change course to port about ninety degrees to blow the soot off the starboard side."

"Not so fast. What will that do to the CPA of our contact?" He raised his voice again. "Goddamn it Harley, you could put us on a collision course."

"Oh, sorry, I guess I'll turn to starboard."

Winthrop stepped back. "Okay, go ahead and change course."

After the maneuver the engine room used compressed air to blow all the soot off the boiler tubes, a regular maintenance action at sea.

As *Eldorado* turned back to its regular course, Winthrop noticed the captain, smiling, get off his perch on the port wing of the bridge and head back to his sea cabin.

And Winthrop saw Johnson grinning. But the second class petty officer put on his cold face as quickly as Winthrop caught the grin. *So maybe the guy can be reached.*

The rest of the watch went smooth. Lee spotted the contact, its hull still below the horizon and just its stack poking into visible range at

26

twelve miles. Larsen made the course change at 1500 after checking first with Winthrop as to the proper protocol for the order to the helm.

At 1600 Tom Randolph with Jay Dunston, relieved Winthrop and Larsen. Dunston, another JG, and third division officer, served as Randolph's JOOD. As gunnery officer he supervised the men who maintained and operated the ship's guns, part of the deck department.

Watches working on a one-in-five rotation, easy duty during the transit, recently went to one-in-four as Mike Appleton, a lieutenant and the communications department head, moved off the rotation. *Eldorado's* communications role in the Vietnam conflict would soon demand his full time attention.

Once in the combat zone the rotation would go to one-in-three and it would be zombie time for Winthrop, Randolph and one other junior officer. The brass had not yet picked him, but probably that officer would be Dunston. Steve Taylor would go back to his full time combat information center officer duties.

~

A week later on a Sunday morning, Winthrop found the captain and the navigator on the bridge when he relived Steve Taylor as OOD. Small islands were visible to port and starboard. Further to starboard the Philippine island of Luzon loomed in the distant midst.

Winthrop walked around, checking out the situation before assuming the watch. *Eldorado's* course had brought her to the San Bernardino Strait, a necessary passage for quickly reaching the west side of the Philippines and continuing to Subic Bay. The bridge radar repeater displayed comma-shaped contacts here and there. No other ships were in view, only a few fishing boats near one of the small islands.

27

Art Chambers, the JOOD, waiting for Larsen to relieve him said, "Those are rips. Cause some trouble sometimes. That's why the old man is here."

"Ought ta make the watch go faster," Winthrop said, "a little action up here, huh?"

He walked over, relieved Randolph, and took the conn.

"Morning, Captain," he said and saluted, it being protocol upon first meeting the captain each day.

Captain Robert Ridgeway, a rangy, fit man with lively blue eyes, returned the salute. "We're taking three-minute fixes, Fred. The current changes quite a bit, and then there are those rips. Carry on as usual. You might have to make a few course changes. Keep the speed at ten knots or less. I'll stay around here awhile if you don't mind."

Winthrop grinned. "It's your ship sir."

The four-striper grunted and walked toward his port chair.

Owen James, the navigator and a senior lieutenant touched Winthrop's arm.

"I'll give ya any course changes." He towered over Fred a good six inches. That and his bald head gave him a dominating appearance. The popular officer could deliver a punch line on a joke as well as the best comedians. Now he was serious. From the Deep South, over his years in service he managed to overcome his accent for the most part. "We're being set to port by the current right now."

"Thanks man."

Winthrop walked over to his JOOD, standing by the starboard hatch.

"Harley, I'll hang on to the conn this watch."

Ensign Larsen frowned. "Okay."

28

Flagship

"Don't worry, your day will come." Larsen reminded Winthrop of himself a year and a half before as an ensign, eager to run things.

Jones, at the port lookout station, shouted something and pointed forward. A rip bubbled up under the ship's bow. Smallish, the radar hadn't picked it up.

The helmsman sung out. "Lost steering, sir."

Shit!

"Standby to shift to hand-electric," Winthrop said, an automatic response embedded in his unconscious from countless drills. The shift probably wouldn't solve the problem. The big wheel ran on hydraulics to control the ship and offered the helmsman a feel for the vagaries of the rudder. The automobile-like steering wheel called hand-electric, more like power steering, wouldn't work if the problem was the hydraulic lines. Electric servos on the smaller wheel operated the same hydraulic lines to the rudder.

"Shift to hand electric." He gave the order anyway, following drill.

As expected, the helmsman shouted, "Lost steering, sir."

"Standby to shift to after steering," Winthrop said, followed by, "All ahead one- third," to slow the ship down to five knots.

The old man climbed out of his chair and stood watching.

The phone-talker stationed at the engine order telegraph rang up ahead-one-third and sung-out, "After-steering is standing-by, sir."

"Very well. Shift to after steering."

It didn't work.

The passive ocean continued with its currents and rips. Winthrop could see the white streaks around distant islands from foaming surf. *Eldorado's* fate hung in the hands of her crew. Without them, she was a floating hunk of metal.

29

The phone-talker sung out, "Engine room at one-third, sir." Then, "After-steering reports lost steering. They can't get the pins in for manual."

The captain spoke. "I'll take the conn, Mister Winthrop."

"Aye, sir. The captain has the conn," Winthrop shouted out.

"Shall I notify the signal bridge, sir?

"Yes," the captain said, then, "Boats get the Chief Engineer up here."

Johnson, at the ready by the 1 MC, blew his pipe and announced. "Chief engineer to the bridge, Chief engineer to the bridge, on the double."

Winthrop, on the 21 MC said, "Signal bridge, conn, run up the not-under-command shapes."

"Signal bridge, Aye." They would run up two large black ball-shaped signals on the ship's signal lines, notifying any ships in the area that *Eldorado* could not maneuver.

"What have we got, Navigator." the old man addressed James.

"Open water 'bout three miles to port and eight miles to starboard, suh." James's southern accent came out under stress.

The old man frowned. "Damn, we're being set to port too."

"Recommend we back, Sir," Winthrop said.

The captain, an *airdale*, who made his reputation as a torpedo plane pilot in World War Two, and who was now experiencing his first deep-draft command, considered.

"Yeah, okay. "All stop."

The talker rang up *all stop*, then said, "Engine room reports *all stop*."

Winthrop had moved to the revolutions per minute gage on the forward bulkhead.

Flagship

After a couple of minutes he reported. "Revolutions at zero, sir."

"Very well, all back one-third," Ridgway said, followed by, "all back two thirds."

The chief engineer arrived, puffing. "Need me sir."

"Get the goddamn steering fixed now, Ed."

Ed McCullough, a mustang lieutenant, shorter than Winthrop, with lively eyes and a buck tooth grin, knew the engineering business and the ship's systems as well as anyone in the shipyard that built it. He went to work. He dialed the department office on the ship's phone and ordered a bunch of pipefitters to the steering gear compartment. They found the hydraulic break and fixed it.

When they reported the fix to the bridge McCullough said, "Those hydraulic lines are old, your rip current forced the rudder to move, pushed the pressure backwards, and busted one. Probably won't happen again."

Winthrop parked that bit of information deep back in his brain, with a different take. *Don't trust the rudder. Treat it with care.*

The rest of Winthrop's watch passed with no incident. The Captain retired to his sea cabin and things calmed down as the ship exited the strait.

~

The watch rotation included the "dog-watches" at 1600 to 1800 and then 1800 to 2000, short watches established so watch-standers could get dinner. Thus Winthrop found himself on the bridge again for the 2000 to 2400 watch.

Owen James finished plotting the ship's course up toward Subic on the wheelhouse chart table, stretched, and spotted Winthrop as he

31

assumed the watch. He caught up with Winthrop on the wing of the bridge. "See those fires over on the beach," he said.

Flickers of light danced on the distant shoreline to starboard. Filipino fisherman anchored for the night. Far from most modern conveniences, they lived closer to nature and fished for their livelihood. Fish and rice for meals, far from the war machines, permanently balmy weather by the sea, except for storms, not a bad life.

James chuckled. "I told Johnson they were KKK fires. Man you shoulda seen his eyes. He asked, 'They got the Klan out here?'"

Not so funny. Winthrop laughed his courtesy laugh, and walked back into the wheelhouse. James headed down to the wardroom to see the movie.

~

Johnson

Johnson moved to the 1 MC, blew his pipe and announced; "Now de movieee . . . in de wardrooooom be De Ghost and Mesteer Chicken. De movieee . . . on de mess deck be de incredible Mr. Limpet."

Screw James.

Johnson thought his recital in Deep South black lingo of the movie title ought to make his point. And Winthrop, Johnson heard the navigator tell him the joke. Winthrop should have said something. *He laughed.* The officers made a point that all the sailors were equal. But Johnson doubted that. Only a black man could kid around with him like that. James wasn't his friend.

What could they do? Put him on report? For what? His wife's admonishment came back to him. *Watch your temper, Jerome.*

They could do a lot. Not formally, he realized but informally. They could need him in the master at arms department, the ship's policemen, taking him off the watch bill. He relished his bridge watches. Or, they could need him back in the PBRs.

Better cool it.

~

Crap, now what. Johnson, who spoke normal English, delivered the announcement over the whole ship with the heaviest black Southern accent in Winthrop's experience.

The movies were lousy, no first run movies for the crew until the combat zone. That was bad enough, but now what the hell to do about his boatswain, Winthrop thought.

The executive officer, Commander Webster, burly, dark hair, balding, came wandering out on the weather deck. Not a coincidence, Winthrop thought. *Shit.* He stepped through the hatch back out to the weather deck.

"Nice evening, huh, Fred," the commander said, keeping his normal booming voice low.

"Beautiful," Winthrop said.

"Who's your boatswain's mate of the watch?"

"Johnson, sir."

"I see. Carry on."

He turned and walked back to his cabin situated on the port side behind the wheelhouse and the quartermaster shack, and opposite the captain's sea cabin. The XO answered to the captain for all personnel issues.

This wasn't over.

Winthrop walked over to Lee at the port lookout station. "How's things?" He said.

Lee put on that look, lidded eyes and all. "It be jes fine, sur."

33

Shit.

The watch dragged as Winthrop stewed. He walked around the bridge appearing to check things, his unsettled mind stuck on the two black sailors under his supervision. He gave the conn to Larsen early on. Larsen managed to handle it without screwing up. It helped that the ship needed no course or speed changes.

At 2200 Johnson piped, "Taps! Taps! Out all white lights. All hands turn in to their racks and maintain silence about the decks. Taps." He used regular English.

At 2400 Winthrop's relief showed up and Winthrop had not acted on Johnson's behavior at all. *Maybe that's best, let it go.*

He took the outside route down to officer's country. The soft breeze, warm on his face, the half-moon illumination of the sea, the quiet slushing of the water along the hull, and the friendliness of light shining from open portholes, belayed the human concerns of *Eldorado's* embarked crew. Winthrop headed for the sack.

4

The following morning, January 31, after a breakfast of poached eggs on toast, home fries, and coffee, Winthrop heard the 1 MC boatswain's call, "Now station the special sea and anchor detail."

His normal watch wouldn't have come up until noon but as sea and anchor detail OOD he now stood on the bridge with the captain and the harbor pilot. The ship had passed Grande Island where the pilot boarded and now the tugs pushed her toward the pier. The subtle odor of rotting seaweed and saltwater announced their arrival at the Subic Bay Naval base. The pilot talked to the tug skippers on a walkie-talkie and gave directions to the old man who relayed them in the form of orders to the helm, engine room, and sailors on deck.

The pilot and the captain, standing by the compass binnacle next to the port lookout, continued to direct the berthing. Winthrop strode to the starboard to watch as *Eldorado* slowly moved sideways toward her sister ship, the USS *Estes,* where she would tie up.

~

Winthrop's thoughts wandered. He recalled the day in 1965 when he first reported to *Eldorado*, at the same pier, as a new ensign. Having finished officer candidate school in Newport, Rhode Island, the previous August, he received orders to *Eldorado,* but first, the Navy sent him to combat information center school until mid-December.

After home leave for Christmas, he flew out to San Francisco, took a cab to Travis Air Force Base, found the payroll office, got a cash travel supplement, took a space in the bachelor officers' quarters for the night and the next day boarded a military charter jet for the Philippines.

His previous experience flying alone had been short Mohawk Airlines flights home from college.

At the time, he viewed the whole thing as an adventure, like college students who go off to Europe or tour America for a year before settling down and getting a job.

Funny how adventurous this stuff seemed when you thought you were immortal.

He arrived at Clark Air Base near Manila hours later and stepped down into a muggy sauna. Base personnel assigned him a room in the bachelor officer quarters. The next morning he joined several other military guys on a bus to Subic Bay. After a slow, hot ride on winding jungle covered rural roads, it dropped him outside the gate of the US Naval Station. Hot, lugging his heavy navy blue canvass duffle, uncomfortable in his sweat-soaked khaki uniform, he flustered his way to the gate. Eager, he saluted some sort of official, who he later figured to be a chief, a faux pas, but understandable for a twenty-two-year-old, inexperienced ensign. The chief, with a straight face, hailed a passing public works pick-up and directed the Filipino driver to drop Winthrop at the *USS Eldorado.*

"Welcome to RPI," the driver said and grinned, showing several gold teeth.

'Hot," Winthrop said.

"Not so bad," the driver said.

At the pier Winthrop stepped out of the cab, reached into the truck bed, retrieved his bag, and stared. Sobered by the sight of her, he paused for a moment. She was no cruiser or destroyer, her lines more like a large merchant ship. The vessel would be his home for the next three years, enduring what she endured, for his full active duty commitment.

Flagship

Winthrop already knew her stats. At 460 feet, her length exceeded a football field, her beam spanned 63 feet. She carried a 5"/38 gun on the bow along with twin 40-millimeter guns for defense, forward of the bridge on both sides. A helicopter landing platform filled her stern, an accommodation for the admiral. Antennas of all descriptions rose from various places in her superstructure. She housed a crew of 450 plus 50 or more men assigned to the admiral's staff.

Winthrop stumbled up the steel stairway, which he learned to call the brow, to the quarterdeck and as trained, saluted the flag at the stern, turned, saluted the officer of the deck and said, "Ensign Winthrop reporting for duty, Sir."

What a start. The rest was a blur in his spinning head, but he recalled the OOD, another ensign dressed in whites, entered his reporting time and date in the log: noon, December 31, 1965. His new year would start aboard ship.

Sometime between that date, when he was more of a civilian, dressed as a Navy officer, and the present, he left his college plans, all his youthful ambitions, and became Mister Winthrop. The new jargon, new duties, new friends, a new life, and an awareness of his own mortality sobered him.

~

Winthrop's reverie stopped when the boatswain piped, "The officer of the deck is moving his watch to the quarterdeck." That meant Winthrop was off duty as less senior officers stood the in-port quarterdeck watches.

Liberty Call sounded and scores of white hats scurried down the after-brow, destination, the city of Olongapo, which some called the pearl of the Orient. Others used more descriptive names. No stopping the liberty hounds, from *Eldorado's* deck, the sailors would hit town, find a dive, and sit, San Miguel beer bottles in hand, smiling bar-girls on their laps, grins on their faces, in an interval an observer could measure in minutes.

"Hey sailor, I love you no-shit, buy me a drink," was the operative phrase for the girls of Olongapo.

On the following day, the admiral shifted his flag to *Eldorado.* His entourage of officers and men moved in to the staff quarters, one deck above the ship's company officers country. The admiral himself took the next deck topside, just under the captain's and XO's quarters, and the navigation bridge. *Estes* headed for the states. Winthrop's vessel took *Estes* place next to the pier.

~

A ceremony marking the movement of the rear admiral, who held the operating title of commander amphibious forces pacific fleet, ensued on the next morning. It involved a perfunctory inspection of all hands.

After breakfast, on a sunny and humid but not yet broiling forward boat deck, Winthrop found himself in dress whites standing in front of first division waiting for the captain and admiral to make their way to his men. He took the moment to check their appearance. All but one, impeccable in their uniforms, stood smartly as he walked around them.

The one exception Winthrop knew as Seaman Earnest Mayer, called by the other sailors "Weasel." With a sly but weak smile and downcast eyes the man stood before him at five feet, six, in oversized white pants, no belt and a stained top, his hat the grayish color of a worn sneaker.

Flagship

"What kind of uniform is that?" Winthrop said more in puzzlement than anger. *Why would a man come to inspection dressed like that?*

Winthrop inspected him. English blue eyes contrasted with dark brown hair. Mayer's weak countenance belied his sturdy build. When a man lacked confidence yet displayed a robust physique, in Winthrop's view, the cause could be found in mental or emotional issues.

"They stole my stuff," Mayer said. "This is all I could find."

"Get below," Winthrop said. "I don't want the captain to see you like that. Stay in your compartment 'til I send for you. Christ man."

He went over to Nobel, leaned in his face. "What the fuck is Mayer doing up here dressed like that?"

"Thought you should see it, sir. Some of the guys swiped all his gear. Payback ya know. He always steals, ya know."

Winthrop stepped back, considering.

"You had trouble with him before, I recall."

"The scrub brush shower straightened out his hygiene problem."

"No details please." Winthrop didn't want to know about the shower scrub with stiff brushes, the unwritten Navy answer to crewmembers that didn't wash. If he knew and did not report it, he could be court martialed, along with his first class and his best sailors. Christ, Winthrop thought, he never would have authorized that. Nobel had only hinted about the midnight shower lesson, not enough detail for Winthrop to be sure it occurred. He had to admit; whatever they did, Mayer now kept himself clean with regular showers.

"What's his problem?" Winthrop said.

"Don't know. He's screwed up though."

39

"After the inspection, round up some old work denims for him to wear and bring him up to the office."

The inspection progressed as such ceremonies do. Rather than search for problems at such events the brass used inspections to build morale and pride in service. Deficiencies of such obvious nature as Mayer's uniform would bring a rebuke to the division officer. Winthrop had sidestepped a near certain reprimand.

He suspected Mayer of sneak theft. Once he woke before a mid-watch to spot Mayer going through his stateroom desk. Mayer, messenger-of-the-watch for the eight to twelve, had a reason to be in his room to wake him, make sure he could relieve the OOD on time. Sleepy and not sure what he saw, Winthrop said nothing but registered the event in his memory.

Nobel brought the sailor up to the deck office in the afternoon. The man, shaking, tears in his eyes, stood, holding a dirty old hat, and wearing torn denims Nobel had scrounged.

"Let's go topside," Winthrop said as Joe Trucker gave him a look.

Randolph and Dunston, fellow division officers, their desks situated across from Winthrop in the same office, turned at their chairs.

On the main deck, Winthrop led the two forward past the admiral's barge up near the anchor chains with a view of the dock.

"So what's going on," Winthrop said, addressing Mayer.

"They stole my uniforms."

"You know who?"

"No, sir. I don't have no money to buy more, sir. I send most home to my mother. She ain't got nobody but me, sir."

"Where you from?"

"North Carolina." He spoke with the slightest hint of an accent.

40

Winthrop turned to Nobel, "Any ideas?"

"Beats me who did it, sir."

"Whose his leading petty officer?"

"Bode, sir."

"Find Bode. You and Bode bring Mayer to the chaplain. See if he has a fund or something to buy a new set of uniforms. And Nobel, take him off messenger duties. Assign him to my watch section as starboard lookout. Belcher's been there a while. You can start him training on the helm."

~

Mayer

What else could I do, the bastards stole my uniforms. Mayer thought of his mom. Much of his pay went to her as an allotment. He signed up for the maximum allotment. The chaplain had been kind to him, bought him some new uniforms at the navy exchange, and got him assigned to a first division berthing compartment.

Mayer knew who stole his uniforms, but didn't turn them in. Those second division guys did it. *Weasel,* they called him. Well he was a first division sailor but because of some quirk was assigned to a second division berthing compartment. They picked on him since he came aboard. Sullivan, they called him Sully initiated it all.

On the transit, Mayer had taken to sleeping in the forward rope locker. No one bugged him there and he could arrange the rope coils to sleep okay. But they swiped his uniforms, all of them. He figured Sully engineered the deed. He couldn't prove it but Sully had been claiming someone swiped his dress blues top implying it was Mayer. Sometimes Mayer saw some loose change lying around when he made his rounds as

41

messenger of the watch. He took the change. He needed it. But he hadn't taken Sully's uniform.

~

Winthrop didn't care much for the chaplain, a lieutenant commander assigned to *Eldorado*, like the doctor and dentist, because the ship carried an embarked admiral. As far as he could figure the chaplain didn't do much but supervise one yeoman and the ship's library, a tiny compartment attached to his larger office, located among the officers' staterooms. The other thing he did was complain about the lack of proper conduct in the wardroom, or decorum as he called it, something the junior officers tended to violate rather often.

Put the man to work, Winthrop reasoned, that was his job, not just the charity part. The fine line between physiological counseling and spiritual counseling in Winthrop's view meant if he were to make a good sailor out of Mayer, the chaplain should help.

~

In early evening Fred Winthrop, Tom Randolph, and Jay Dunston, dressed in their civvies, prepared to take Harley Larsen out on the town. They met him by his stateroom putting on some Canoe.

"Ya don't need cologne here, Harley," Jay said, "just cash."

"Don't we need pesos? Where do we get those?" He said.

"We can buy some at the gate. Come on," Winthrop said.

What had once been a clear jungle stream but now carried urban runoff from town ran between the base and Olongapo. Poor families in ramshackle boats stationed under the bridge held up their hands and begged. The four officers obliged with some coins.

After crossing the stench-enveloped river they arrived on Magsaysay Avenue. The best way to describe the street, Winthrop

42

thought, was like Avenue Revolution in Tijuana on a Saturday night, wild, wooly, and multiplied ten-fold. The sheer abundance of bar girls, outnumbered only by drunken sailors and junior officers, made the street unique in Southeast Asia. Bars and cheap hotel rooms, rentable by the hour lined the street.

Garish neon lights advertised sexy girls, liquor, and dancing to rock 'n roll, country, and jazz. Jeepneys buzzed up and down the street. A four-man shore patrol contingent wandered through the jumble of humanity, conspicuous, almost self-conscious in demeanor.

A man stood on a corner hawking *baloot*, fertilized duck eggs boiled just before hatching and sold throughout the Philippines as aphrodisiacs. Winthrop always thought of the tidbit as a bad joke played on unsuspecting American sailors.

Randolph started in. "Hey, Harley, bet you can't eat a baloot."

"You ever eat one, Tom," Larsen said.

"Hell no, but I'll buy all your beer tonight if ya can get one down."

A couple of drunken sailors in uniform strutted up to the vendor. "I'll try a baloot," one said. "I'm not a wimpy officer."

He bought one and cracked the shell. A tiny bill and fluff of tiny feathers peeked out at him. Steeling himself, he wolfed it down in a few chews and a gulp. Shortly he barfed in some bushes nearby.

His buddy laughed.

The four wimpy officers roared as the two sailors made their way back toward the gate.

"They'll need help even finding their ship." Winthrop said when the laughter died down.

They spent the rest of the evening trying seedy bars, ending up in the "Pride of the Fleet" night club. Dim lights hide the grime on the floor but a young man with a rag and a bucket kept the tables and chairs clean and dry. The quiet crowd allowed them to talk. Dunston with a girlfriend in the states, stuck to nursing a beer and fiddling with the candle lamp at the center of the table. Larsen and Randolph enjoyed the blandishments of two sexy bar girls, buying them "drinks" which consisted of iced tea masquerading as bourbon and water.

Music from a jute box played soft dreamy ballads for the remaining customers, enticing them to join their dancing partners for the night at one of the hotels along the avenue.

"These Filipino chicks are okay," Dunston said, "but nothing beats a pretty round eye."

"American girl," the girl sitting on Larsen's lap said, "all talk no action. You sailors, always 'slam, bam, thank you ma'am.' American girls frigid, not for you. This Filipina no round eye. You treat good, she treat you good."

"Didn't mean you," Dunston said, "just homesick."

"Don't grump. Pick girl. Take her to hotel. She make you forget."

Dunston, a low key, easy going, chronic complainer, shrugged and shook his head.

"Good man Jay," Winthrop said. "But you aren't married or anything. Bet your girl's out right now playing WESTPAC widow with some Marine."

"Ya never met her, Fred. She wrote me a lot of letters. They caught up with me yesterday when we got our mail."

"Well, maybe she is the one. I'll back you up when we get home. Tell her you didn't mess around."

Winthrop stayed with Dunston for three beers, then succumbed to a pretty Filipina, and left Dunston soaking in his loneliness.

44

Flagship

~

The following morning the regulars at Winthrop's table, Chips Beasley and Merlin Chandler, the two W-4 warrant officers, along with Jay Dunston, Tom Randolph, and Harley Larsen kicked around the previous night's adventures. Beasley and Chandler, old married men, prodded the guys for details; Beasley to tease, Chandler to admonish.

Ol' Chips moved in. "Ya guys gonna be ready for the Captain's short arm inspection when we head home after the tour aren't ya?"

All but Larsen knew at the end of the cruise all hands would be offered a voluntary urine and blood test to clear up any undetected cases of VD. True to sailors' proclivity for hyperbole, it became known as "the short arm inspection."

Larsen's face dropped.

Now rolling, Chips gave Larsen a hard look. "Ya realize the old man knows which of his officers been consortin'. At the end of this tour you gotta stand naked in ranks so's the medical officer can inspect ya for 'Vietnamese Rose.'"

Larsen, perspiration bubbles appearing on his face, could manage only a "huh?"

Merlin Chandler pontificated, "Those prostitutes will only bring you trouble. Best to stay away like Jay."

Jay Dunston started a slow grin, coming out of his funk.

"You been there, Merlin?" he said.

"Of course. I was young once. Listen and learn."

"Vietnamese Rose," Larsen said, "what's that?" wet stains growing under his arms.

"Guys brought it to the RPI from 'Nam. Can slip through a rubber. Ain't curable, doesn't affect ya much at first, 'cept you grow this

45

canker on your you-know-what. Looks like a rose, all red an' everthin.'
Hard to keep the ladies from seein' it, ya know."

Chandler began to shake his head. Ocampo, the Filipino steward
for the table, hovered nearby listening as Chips weaved his story.
Winthrop put his milk glass down.

"So ya see the only thing happens as it heals," Chips said. "It
starts drying up, gettin' wrinkly an all. Seems to have run its course, you
know."

The Chipper paused, raising his head, his rimless spectacles
glinting in the morning sun's rays pouring through the wardroom
portholes.

"Then your dick falls off."

The guys roared. Even Larsen chimed in. "Okay Chips, You got
me."

Ocampo ran back to the galley to share the story with the other
stewards.

The chaplain rose to half-standing at the XO's table, his napkin
tucked in his belt squeezed belly, harrumphed, frowned and stared.
Winthrop's table roared.

The XO, struggling to remain serious, stood. "Now gentlemen,"
he said.

5

That evening, Winthrop skipped the Olongapo scene and walked to the O club with Jay Dunston and Joe Trucker. Joe, a married man, and Jay with a girlfriend in the states, had good reason. Fred Winthrop wanted a couple beers, not another raucous night out.

They sat at the glossy mahogany and brass bar and played "captain and crew" for drinks. The cleanliness of the club put it far above the Olongapo night clubs in class, but it lacked the female companionship available in town. The few women who showed up at the place were wives of officers stationed on the base. The sparse sprinkling of patrons, all male, signified the early hour. Jay lost the dice game. He grumbled something about a run of bad luck.

"Come on Jay," Winthrop said, "you got a round-eye chick back home hot for your bod."

He grinned. "She's not here." He nodded toward the hostess standing at the restaurant entrance. "There's something you don't see much in the RPI. Must be a wife of some guy stationed here."

"Don't see a ring," Winthrop said, noticing the American woman for the first time. "I'll go talk to her."

She stood straight, poised, and composed as Winthrop approached. Wavy, dark blond hair, tall, five foot eight or nine, he figured. She wore light make-up, struck a trim athletic figure, not too big on top, slim waist.

"Quiet evening in the restaurant?" Winthrop said.

Her eyes appraised him. She cocked her head.

"Do you want a table," she said.

47

No, I want you.

Aloud, he said, "Can I buy you a cup of coffee when you get off?"

"I don't know you."

"I'm off the *Eldorado*, single, harmless."

"I never met a harmless junior officer," her eyes joining her month in a flirty smile.

"Come on we'll have fun."

"Okay, I'm off in an hour. What about your buddies?" She turned her head toward Trucker and Dunston.

"They're taken, women at home."

Head down, she smiled, more to herself than at Winthrop. "What's your name?"

"Fredrick Winthrop the Third. Call me Fred."

An older couple approached the restaurant and Fred walked back to the bar.

~

After an hour Trucker and Dunston moved to the slot machine to kill some time before heading back to the ship. Winthrop found his lady walking from the restaurant and guided her to a table.

"I didn't get your name," he said.

"Mary Litton. My dad's the base commander."

"My dad served in the Navy too. Retired now."

"Daddy's on his last tour, passed over for admiral. Mom's been lonely and my brother's a pilot on *Kitty Hawk*, so I took off a semester from college to spend some time here."

"Why work at the club?"

"It's part-time. Just moved here and took the job for something to do."

48

"Must get a lot of dates."

"You're the first."

"Working tomorrow?"

"No, I don't work Fridays, only Wednesdays and Thursdays for a couple of hours."

"Lucky me you were here," Winthrop said. "How about I pick you up tomorrow morning?"

"You'll have to meet Daddy."

~

Friday morning after muster and officer's call, Joe Trucker signed Winthrop's one-day leave chit only after razzing him about chasing the first round eye skirt he found.

By ten, sporting a new white *barong,* the long, lightweight shirt of the Philippines, dark blue chinos purchased first thing at the Navy exchange, and shiny black shoes dug out of his locker, Winthrop showed up at the base commander's residence. Sweat popped out on his forehead. *Hot, Winthrop, or scared?*

Captain Litton answered the bell in his whites, smiled. "How'd you get off on a workday? Captain Ridgway's a stickler."

Winthrop took in the man's gold braid on his hat visor, the four gold strips on his solder epaulets, and the five rows of ribbons on his chest. Mary's old man had been around.

"Morning, sir, just got into port. Got one day off, sir. Lots of stuff going on."

"Don't I know? Be good to my daughter, Mister Winthrop." Litton headed out to his jeep.

Mary, wearing sandals and a pale pink dress, light weight, cotton or something, Winthrop figured, walked out of the living room. Tiny beads

49

of sweat on her upper lip defined the Republic of the Philippine Islands climate—hot, dripping humidity.

"Let's go for a walk by the water," Winthrop said.

"How was Daddy?"

"Okay. Four-stripers make me nervous, until I get to know them. Captain Ridgway used to do that. Now I'm relaxed dealing with him."

"You went native fast with the barong."

"The natives got this heat figured out."

Her dress hung from thin straps on delicate, smooth, and soft shoulders. The smoothness continued on her neckline to the slight rounding at the beginning of her beasts.

Their bodies touched as they walked. Winthrop's urges caroused through him. A sense told him the same heat flowed in her. The human condition, Winthrop thought. Primitive cravings melded with emotions. With women he often felt the allure, not with all, but with many. No previous woman had raised him to such intensity. Mary generated his desire like lava from an erupting volcano. Was it nature or the long time at sea?

He took her hand. She squeezed his. They stopped under a spreading Fig tree near The Spanish Gate, a remnant of the days Spain ruled the waves and controlled the Philippines. The fragrance of the abundant flowers surrounding them rivaled their colors for attention. Sprawling blues, velvet and robust reds, brilliant whites and yellows buried in lush greens of all hues.

If ever a moment existed when all possibilities stood before them, Mary and Fred experienced it at that spot. He kissed her. She moved, pressing close. He sensed the urgency of her desire in her hips. He wanted to absorb her and yet still experience the rhythmic pressure from her hips and the softness of her breasts against him. She pulled away.

"God," she breathed.

"Yeah."

They walked and talked some more. An average student studying to be a teacher at Miami University of Ohio, Mary had dated a few casual boyfriends in the past but never met one she cared to commit to. So she broke with them before they got too serious.

A funny thing, Winthrop thought, women as well as men lived with the desire, sometimes overwhelming, for sex. The wise individual avoided situations which began to lead the other person on. Sometimes the happy-stance occurred and a relationship progressed just for sex, and no commitment, but often one party began to experience an emotional attachment. In such cases Winthrop dropped the chick. While it was effortless to become entangled in an undesirable relationship led on by easy sex, hurt feelings healed easier early-on, rather than late and deep into one party's unrealistic dreams.

Mary and Fred stood on the precipice. Better to slow up, he reasoned, than to rush things. The concept stood on one side and all the craving of an evolved man facing a scintillatingly desirable woman stood on the other. Mary's actions so far indicated she harbored the same yearning.

He took her to dinner and walked her home, holding hands. The delicate fuzz on her arms glowed in the moonlight accentuating the creamy glow of the skin beneath. After a memorable kiss he walked back to the ship, his senses sprinting ahead like the high-pitched peak of a symphony crescendo. `

51

Fleet operations required *Eldorado's* presence in the combat zone along the coast of Vietnam. After a couple of weeks of resupply and minor upkeep, essential after the Pacific transit, *Eldorado* would head into the fray.

The schedule allowed Fred and Mary less than two weeks.

6

Joe Trucker came to his table Saturday morning, bent toward Winthrop. "Can I see you for a minute after breakfast?"

Lieutenant Joe Trucker tended toward stoic, taciturn, but not aloof. His close-chopped blond hair reflected his Annapolis training.

"Huh, yeah," Winthrop said.

Winthrop's head buzzed with thoughts of Mary. Memories of their walking, talking, and making out all day Friday burned in his brain. Unfulfilled sex intensified their romance. Winthrop planned to pick her up at her house and take her over to Olongapo during the day to show her the place when things were quiet. He dare not dream of what might happen should they venture into one of the hotels. Their yearnings mutual, their hesitancy mutual, yet they planned an outing with potential for high stake consequences.

After breakfast he and Trucker filled their coffee cups. Winthrop added sugar and evaporated milk, the Navy's answer to the perishability of cream in the tropics. Trucker took his black. They sat in a couple of the wardroom lounge chairs with the coffee mugs.

"Want to talk about Johnson," Trucker said. "XO says Captain's thinking of a transfer for him."

The statement took Winthrop out of his Mary reverie. *Here it comes.*

"With the Martin Luther King situation and the Black Panthers stuff back in the states, the captain's concerned about a racial incident on *Eldorado*." He fingered his chin, a nervous habit of Trucker's.

Winthrop and Trucker maintained a friendly relationship because Trucker trusted his loyalty. Trucker acted more detached with Randolph because Randolph wise-mouthed him a few times in the past. And Dunston was not the type to chat much. Winthrop and Trucker shared a respect for the Navy and its protocols.

"Where would they transfer him?"

"One of the PBRs, chasing gun runners, the Market Time Operation. We're providing communication services for them. He'll be too busy to cause any trouble."

"Shit, man he's done that brown water stuff, survived. He's got a family, does a good job here."

"You know what this is about, Fred?" Trucker said.

"I suspect it's because of his 1 MC movie announcements the other night."

"Yep, I heard it. The whole damn ship heard it. We don't need some sort of civil rights demonstration on this ship, for Christ's sake."

"I doubt it will happen again."

"What do you know, Fred?" Tucker looked at him hard. "Come on, the old man asked me to run this by you, hear your take. It better be good. You know the old man. Nothing, no man, no social issue is more important than our job. We aren't a fuckin' sociological institute. This is the Navy. We don't need some personal vendetta, to cause trouble, racial or whatever."

"Something set him off," Winthrop said. "I'm sure he won't go off again. I can say the circumstances are sensitive. I think it would be detrimental to the Navy, this ship's operations, for me to put the captain in the position of knowing. If he still wants my take, I can tell him."

Trucker paused, rubbed his chin.

54

Flagship

"Another issue," he said. "Mayer's a problem. We can get him off too, before we go over to the war zone. Give him an admin discharge."

"The Navy's all the kid's got. He supports his widowed mother. Sends most of his pay to her. I'd say we take a chance on him. I got him off messenger duties. Hard for him to steal without a reason to be in sleeping areas. His shipmates taught him a lesson."

"You're getting to be a regular bleeding heart, Fred, Christ. Don't know about Johnson, but I can cover you on Mayer. We'll keep him on the ship."

Trucker drained his cup, stood.

"Take your girlfriend over to White Rock Beach," he said. "Skip the town unless you want her to dump you."

~

Mary sat on the porch as Winthrop approached the house. He studied her face. With almost straight eyebrows of dark blond hair, no mascara, natural hair, no artificial stuff, and pretty bangs, she appeared like the classic girl next door. She wore a light-weight dress reaching to her knees. The top exhibited her bare shoulders and a familiar hint of velvet cleavage.

His heart beat picked up. In an attempt to deal with the humidity he wore khaki shorts he found at the exchange, a white polo shirt, and tennis shoes, no socks.

She stood and beamed. "Good morning, Mister Winthrop."

Winthrop's knees fluttered, his voice quivered. "You look lovely this morning, Miss Litton."

The artificial formalities heightened their mutual anticipation of pleasure. He took her hand. She squeezed it. He led her toward the main

55

gate. They strolled in a blissful haze past palm trees and luxurious tropical plants flowering with color.

Leaving the base behind, they crossed the Kalalake River, unaware if its smell, "Shit River," as sailors and marines called it.

He hailed a jitney on the other side. "White Rock Beach," he said.

Mary raised her eyebrow, cocked her pretty head. "Not showing me the town, Mister Winthrop?"

"This is better. We can walk on the beach. You're too nice for this street full of bars."

"Daddy's told me about them."

They boarded the converted jeep and sat close on one of the two bench-like seats stretched out perpendicular to the driver. Gaudy decorated curtains fell a quarter ways from the top making the open-air vehicle appear like a foot carriage of royalty.

Dozens of similar vehicles darted around Olongapo. They didn't notice. They rode in their own bubble simmering with anticipation. They held hands.

The fresh ocean breeze mitigated the humidity when they arrived before noon. Winthrop paid the driver a few pesos, ignored the hotel standing near the shore, and led Mary away toward a secluded spot. They walked near the water. Mary removed her sandals. Winthrop walked a while before removing his shoes. Far down the shore a large group of sailors cavorted on the beach. Some sort of ship's picnic, Winthrop thought.

He led her to a shady spot under a palm tree near the water.

She sat before he could, her dress spread and pulled up revealing creamy thighs. Winthrop took her in. *Beautiful.* Neither wanted to hold back, but they did, once again raising their passions to fever. The distant sailors and beach goers couldn't make out their actions. With ingenuity they could consummate the act. Instead they contented themselves with fervid embrace, a pantomime of the real thing.

The distant hotel beckoned them. They stayed on the sand. They skipped lunch. They skipped dinner. They released all but Fred's passion in complete honesty with each other. Fred's desire ended with an ache for Mary. They rode a jitney back to the base, her head resting on his shoulder.

~

Early Sunday she took Winthrop to church at the base chapel. Mary picked him up on the dock driving her family car. They sat quietly in a pew and listened to a sermon about fear and duty in military service, and God.

After, as she drove him to her house for breakfast with the family she asked, "What did you think?"

"The sermon was fine in the abstract, but not true in reality."

"What do you mean?"

"Nothing's that simple," Winthrop said.

She reached out her hand and touched his knee.

"Well, the two church goers," Mrs. Litton said when they arrived. "Mary doesn't usually go to church since she went off to college."

She led them to the living room where Captain Litton sat reading. A Hawaiian shirt covered his slight paunch, consistent with an active man in his late forties, but his overall appearance Winthrop considered robust.

Wouldn't want to have to fight that man for his daughter.

The captain put his book down as they entered.

"Come set for a minute," he said, "while Sue-Sue sets the breakfast table."

The base commander's large house, befitting a man of his position, but not overwhelming, more like a place in an upper-middle class neighborhood in the States, put Winthrop at ease. Sue-sue, the Filipino maid, lived on the premise.

"Sand Pebbles," Captain Litton said, holding up the book he was reading. "McKenna wrote a paragon. You ever read it, Fred?"

The classic told the story of the old China Fleet and a sailor named Jake Holman who led the life of Riley on a Yangtze River gunboat until the Chinese revolution tore his life into shreds.

"Yes, sir," Winthrop answered, "in college. Got interested when I joined the Navy Reserve."

"Aw . . . so you're a ninety-day wonder like me," the captain said.

"Yes, sir, OCS at Newport."

They ate a breakfast of scrambled eggs, hash browns, bacon, orange juice, and plenty of coffee. The talk at the table involved the Littons questioning Winthrop about his college life. They remained cordial even as he revealed his C-plus average in Business Administration.

Winthrop told them he joined the Navy Reserve in college instead of waiting to see if the draft would catch him after he graduated. He took the student deferment offered all students while in school, but decided to serve as an officer when he graduated.

Some of his contemporaries continued on to graduate school or sped up marriage plans. Both courses offered draft deferments. Others took their chances with the draft.

As an American, Winthrop abhorred the college protesters as cowards. They misrepresented their fear of leaving their soft college lives for the military and justified their actions by frenzied protests against the immorality of the war. Many of the protestors claimed conscientious objection, kissed a draft board member, or otherwise ginned up a reason for the military to reject them. A fair number fled to Canada.

Winthrop's own friends, to a man, supported their country he told the Littons.

Mary spoke little, but smiled often.

After, he and Mary walked and talked. She hold him she thought it unfair that men alone should bear the burden of war. Women, she pointed out, wanted more independence but she never heard her gender advocate being included in the draft. They were hypocrites, she believed. Winthrop liked her clear thinking and firmness, her ability to see the absurdity of things.

They satisfied their undercurrent of need when they found a nook in a group of trees and embraced. He felt the passion as her hips pressed against him.

"This isn't enough," he said.

"I know . . ." she whispered. "I need a little more time."

In the late afternoon Mary drove him back to the ship.

~

Winthrop undressed in his stateroom and headed for the officers' head across the passageway, a cold shower, followed by a hot one, to ease the effects of the heat from the weather and more so, of Mary, on his mind.

Steve Van Valkenburg, an ensign serving in the communications department and Winthrop's roommate in the cramped, two-man space, sat at his desk writing a letter.

"You and your girlfriend don't have much time," Van said.

59

"Huh?"

"Message traffic, can't say much, but we won't be here long."

Van Valkenburg stood watches in a different section, so Winthrop didn't see him much. But "Van" as everyone called him, often handled top secret messages for the admiral's staff as a watch officer in Com.

Van Valkenburg reported to the ship after Christmas, fresh out of communications school, replacing Winthrop's old roommate who was accepted to training in UDT. Winthrop considered underwater demolitions, a volunteer specialty, as a sure way to win medals, but he preferred the relative safety of a ship for his military obligation. Medals helped with one's Navy advancement if one wanted to try for a high rank.

Winthrop had no plans for a Navy career and all the medals in the world wouldn't get him much in civilian life. Perhaps medals should count outside the service, but they didn't. And people soon forgot military daring do, and some disparaged it out of jealousy. Winthrop served because his country needed him. He doubted much demand existed for ship handling in the civilian world. His service amounted to three years of his life donated to his country. Mary was a happy surprise.

"I figure we got two weeks," Winthrop said.

"Might be shorter," was Van's answer. He couldn't say more as Winthrop held only the standard secret clearance of an officer and no "need to know."

7

Someone in the Office of Naval Personnel stymied Nobel's promotion to chief. The unnamed official had "issues" with his recovery from alcoholism, as Commander Webster explained the matter to Trucker and Winthrop. The XO went on to say certain officers would monitor Nobel's behavior during the current deployment and make a final judgement later.

The brass always took the position that no individual's personal situation ranked before accomplishment of the mission of the Navy. A sociologist might belabor the concept, point out the human part of the matter, theorizing that more emphasis on rehabilitating alcoholics would benefit the Navy.

Winthrop knew the brass and the sociologist were both wrong. For the sake of the service, decisions should be made without regard to the problems of individuals. In fact, however, the Navy endured its share of inconsistencies, cronyism, favoritism, and corruption. Nobel's main problem: he lacked connections at BUPERS.

Nobel stood stoic when Winthrop told him about the holdup of his promotion. Then his shoulders slumped.

"I re-enlisted two years ago," he said after standing silent when Winthrop told him the news. "Hoped to make chief and stay in. Guess now I got to get out in two more years, make another life."

"Well, for what it's worth, they're wrong," Winthrop said. "Bet if a Kennedy was in the same predicament, the promotion would go through. Hang in there."

"Thank you sir."

61

Nobel, divorced without children, faced a lonely future. The Navy was his family.

The BUPERS action created repercussions Winthrop hated to deal with. He reasoned if Nobel got through the deployment without hitting the bottle, he might be promoted, but there was no guarantee, and the slap-down from Washington could push Nobel back into the booze. Winthrop needed a strong first class. His own business administration degree didn't equip him with Nobel's technical knowledge and experience in seamanship. From handling the deck booms, the anchor windlass, underway replenishment, and all that, to small craft seamanship, knots, and supervising sailors, Nobel understood it all.

The week passed too fast. He saw Mary every evening. Winthrop's work days heaped full of paperwork and personnel huddles with Nobel, Johnson, and his third-class petty officers. The work load intensified daily as the lady identified as *Eldorado* readied herself to get underway.

~

Johnson brought Seaman Zack Lee to the deck office Friday morning. Both held their hats in hand. Johnson composed, with no black swagger. Lee, head down, eyes on Winthrop, jiggled his hat.

"What's up?" Winthrop said, noting the men's posture and demeanor.

"Lee wants to strike for lithographer's mate, sir."

Reilly, the print shop supervisor, a first class who worked for Winthrop the year before when Winthrop supervised OA Division, needed a new man. He put out the word on the mess decks, and Lee jumped at the chance. The division, which Ensign Larsen supervised, provided print and other support services to the admiral's staff and Navy ships in the area.

Winthrop eyed them both, Johnson's movie announcement replaying in his mind. Prior to World War II black men worked only as cooks or stewards on US Navy ships. Other ratings opened up during the war years, some by formal decree, and some by happenstance. In the fifties Filipinos in the citizenship program replaced most of the black stewards. By the Vietnam era all ratings stood open to all races but white men remained a large majority in key Navy fields. Although blacks did move into the deck ratings and some engineering ratings, many blacks still served as cooks and laundry men. The more arcane fields remained white.

Was this a potential incident of the type that worried the old man?

Striking for a rating, aside from acceptance to one of the special schools run by the Navy, remained the traditional way to move into a specialty from the general category of seaman. Like any job in the civilian world, current supervisors in each field preferred strikers with experience. Printing was a small field for sailors. Easy duty, some said. Sailors found the rating hard to enter.

"Always like to see a man who wants to advance," Winthrop said.

"I got the know-how," Lee said. "An' I been studyin.'"

Winthrop forgot about Mary, his mind dancing on eggshells. Johnson's eyes took on that lidded expression.

"You talk to Reilly?" Winthrop said.

"Want you to," Johnson said.

Johnson pulled Randolph's empty chair over by Winthrop, and sat leaning forward his dark eyes steady, challenging. "It's an opportunity for a black man," he said.

Winthrop visualized a vat of deep shit yawning before him. Damned if I do and damned if I don't.

Johnson's voice sped up and grew a bit louder. He outlined Lee's experience in technical high school back in the States and said Lee had completed the lithographer correspondence course. He expected the certificate when the mail bag arrived.

"I'll give it a shot," Winthrop said, the sweat in his arm pits staining his fresh khaki shirt.

First, Nobel blocked from promotion to chief; next, I get myself into babysitting a thief, and now this.

~

Several decks below the main deck, forward of the engine room, Winthrop found Reilly at his desk in the print shop, feet up, leaning back in the gray chair, and reading *Playboy* as the large printer ran, making a clackity-clack noise. Two of his men attended to the machine as it printed some sort of publication. The shop included a small offset printer, an old fashioned hand press, an embosser, and other equipment, along with the newspaper sized behemoth the two lithographer mates operated.

"We're running off copies of the *Underway Replenishment Manual* for the admiral," he said. "He wants them delivered to all the ships in the Amphibious Ready Group."

"The ARG, huh," Winthrop said. "That means us, and we'll be at sea a long time."

"I'd say."

Flagship

Eldorado's admiral commanded Task Force 76, the Navy's designation for The Amphibious Forces, Pacific Fleet, a major portion of which consisted of the ARG, called in Navy parlance, Task Group 76.4. A Marine Battalion stationed on the ARG's ships could land anywhere along the coast of Vietnam on twenty-four hours notice.

"Hey, Reilly," Winthrop said. "I got a man, wants to strike for the open slot in your shop."

"I got one too. Sullivan, out of second division."

"An Irishman, huh?"

"So what's wrong with an Irishman?"

"What's his qualification? My guy finished the correspondence course and learned the trade in high school."

"I know about your guy, buddies with Johnson. We never had a black man in any print shop where I worked. Maybe Johnson is up to something. And I hear the talk on the mess decks. I don't need a sailor with a chip on his shoulder."

"Johnson's got the chip. Lee's a hard worker. Be good for you. The guys will like him."

Lithographer mate first-class Brandon H. Reilly, a squat, redheaded Irishman, wore his spectacles on his nose as a prop. They kept officers at bay, making him appear more of an expert. He spouted his share of BS, but understood the printing craft more than anyone else on the ship.

"Look, sir, you and I got along okay when you were my division officer. Ya know me. I got no problem with a black man in my shop, but Sully knows his stuff too. His division officer recommended him."

"Give it some thought I'll ask Larsen and the ops boss about it."

I'll ask Randolph what's up too.

65

~

Work occupied Winthrop's mind as he headed off the brow toward the base commander's house.

She met him on the porch in shorts, flip-flops and a revealing yellow top.

"Mom and Dad went to the club for a meet and greet with Admiral Johnson," she said. "He's here on some sort of fact-finding tour. They'll be gone a long time. I made dinner for us."

In the long chain of command to Washington, Admiral Johnson, head of the US Pacific Fleet or CINCPACFLT, stood close to the top. For Winthrop, that didn't matter so much as that *they'll be gone a long time*.

The burgers and fries warmed on the stove, but Fred and Mary moved inside and found the living room couch more beckoning. The "little more time" Mary needed passed into history as their mutual passions overwhelmed them. They embraced with desperation, like the consummation of their love demanded completion or the world would end. The second time occurred soon after, relaxed and caring, and confirmed their relationship on its deep emotional level.

They showered, dressed and ate the burgers. Mary poured wine. They moved to the porch, talking. Fred told her of his division personnel problems and his choice between the strict, Navy-first concept and his instinct.

"Daddy's like that, 'the Navy comes first and all.' Say's I'm too idealistic. When I get older I'll appreciate his wisdom."

"Maybe he's right."

"He didn't make admiral."

He touched her hand. It was enough. They moved inside and made love once more.

66

He left her with a promise to return the next morning.

8

Saturday, at the 0800 Officers' Call, Commander Webster announced the cancellation of all liberty.

"We'll get underway at 0900 tomorrow," he said. "Prepare your departments today. We'll have more information when we are underway."

Winthrop reached the quarterdeck phone, one of only a couple outside lines set up for the ship as two sailors disconnected it.

"Orders, sir," one said.

Van Valkenburg, standing officer of the deck duty, eyed Winthrop. "Sorry man." He had known it was coming.

Winthrop walked forward to find Nobel, thinking to get the duty driver to take him over to Mary's. He found Bode supervising some men operating the ten-ton boom as it removed the heavy cover to auto storage, the large forward hold of the flagship. Nobel stood off in the corner.

"Gotta load the vehicles first thing, sir," Nobel said. "Most of the deck force will be needed on a congo-line at 1030. Supplies coming aboard for sea on the after-brow."

Swallowing annoyance at Nobel's tendency to take charge without checking with him first, Winthrop nodded. He couldn't refute the logic.

"Very well. Carry on," he said. Nobel would catch the irritation in Winthrop's officiousness.

Mary would pick up the news of *Eldorado's* departure from her father. Winthrop figured he gave up his option in this circumstance when he committed to the Navy for three years active duty. Mary would

Flagship

understand, but her last words to him resonated: "Don't forget me in the morning." It had been in jest, but Winthrop hated leaving her with any doubt about returning.

Winthrop headed below toward the deck office. Evidence of the wisdom of the ship's sudden departure met him. He found a bunch of liberty chits on his desk from sailors wanting to visit "girlfriends" on the beach. The "girlfriends" best not learn the flagship was heading out. If they knew, North Vietnam would know. He declined all the chits and put them in Nobel's basket.

He overheard Trucker and Dunston talking. The senior watch officer had refused to recommend Dunston for OOD and for some obscure reason moved Lieutenant Taylor into the OOD watch rotation again.

Dunston, red faced, pissed, said, "I spent time learning the ship. I didn't *gun-deck* my JO Journal."

The brass required new junior officers on *Eldorado* to complete the orientation laid out in a manual of questions to be answered about the various departments on the vessel. The idea was, once the manual was completed the officer "knew the ship." For some reason the current operations department head and senior watch officer ignored cheaters. He compared the individual's responses to the answer sheet and checked off the manual's completion for the officer's record.

As a result a majority of the junior officers learned nothing about the operations of departments other than their own. Most new ensigns on the flagship were ninety-day wonders with no career ambitions other than to complete their draft obligation, so they copied answers from predecessors. If the ops boss didn't know the answers existed on a cheat sheet passed down for years, he was either thick or didn't care. Winthrop figured both reasons to be accurate. Winthrop had finished his JO Journal the hard way and so had Dunston, giving both an advantage of knowledge for use as bridge watch officers.

Winthrop interrupted Trucker and Dunston.

"How about talking to Edgar?" Winthrop said. "Get Jay assigned to my watch and move Larsen to Taylor's section. They're in Edgar's department."

Lieutenant Commander Millard H. Edgar the thick-headed operations department head supervised Taylor and Larsen.

"You don't like Larsen?" Trucker said.

"He's okay but shouldn't be on the bridge. Gun-decked his JO Journal. Ought to spend some time in the combat information center and learn something before the bridge. Jay knows it all. He should be an OOD."

"Let Taylor deal with Harley Larsen if the senior watch officer wants him on the bridge. They're all in the same department. Anyway Taylor runs CIC for Edgar. Maybe he can get him to pull Larsen off the bridge."

The combat information center, or CIC, provided vital long range sensory information, a real asset on many ships. By tradition the operations officer, Lt. Cdr. Edgar in *Eldorado's* case, took the seat as *evaluator* in CIC during general quarters. CIC housed an array of radar repeaters, a dead reckoning tracer, and electronic countermeasures equipment useful in a modern all-out war.

North Vietnam made up for its ground war based WWII vintage weapons with large numbers of troops. Their small navy consisted of patrol type boats and they had no air force. Threats against the flagship came from small craft and swimmers when anchored at remote areas, giving CIC on *Eldorado* little value.

Ship on-scene intelligence defaulted to the bridge. Although Winthrop subscribed to the theory that the old mark-4 eyeball remained the most valuable sensory device at sea, he often ruminated on the vulnerability of relying solely on bridge sources. But a viable facility required firm leadership. Instead, Edger kept his CIC officer tied up in bridge watches. Discipline and leadership slid into complacency and bridge watch officers relied more and more on their own topside resources. The uselessness of CIC amounted to a failure by the ops boss, whom Winthrop saw as a go-through-the-motions officer.

Winthrop gave up on CIC not long after his appointment as an officer of the deck. Drills and various calls for information to the center too often resulted the equivalent of a "huh" for an answer.

Winthrop believed use of the dead reckoning tracer or DRT as they called it, would improve the information for the bridge. The device moved a symbol for the ship in real time across a sheet of continuous paper upon which the radarmen plotted contacts minute by minute. With the device they produced a miniature moving picture of the area for miles around the flagship. They could relay information like course and speed of other ships on demand from the bridge,

Winthrop and the other OODs could figure out that stuff on the bridge by-the-seat-of-their-pants. He had learned the basics of vectors on printed forms called maneuvering boards at OCS. Long hours on the bridge developed the skill so he could now use vectors and a grease pencil to calculate course and speed directly on the radar repeater.

CIC could provide a useful service operating the DRT at all times, thus relieving busy bridge officers of making the calculations. In crowded waters the OODs and JOODs often spent watches hustling from one side of the bridge to the other to keep track of things. Traffic at night in the combat zone ratcheted up the number of contacts and possible threats making heavy demands on their skills.

To Winthrop's constant irritation CIC guys rarely turned on the DRT, and when they did it often broke down.

Trucker interrupted Winthrop's line of thought. "I'll talk to Mister Edgar. No problem. Jay's on your watch from now on."

He turned to Dunston. "I'll work on Edgar to recommend you, Jay. I think you're ready."

He wagged his finger at Winthrop.

"Fred, you lucked out. The old man dithered so long on transferring Johnson. It's too late. Johnson stays. No transfer to the PBRs."

"Dithered?"

"That was the XO's exact word. Don't repeat that. Guess your take gave him some doubts. But if I know Ridgway, ya better hope Johnson stays outta trouble."

~

After Sunday breakfast, Winthrop went topside past the quarterdeck and forward to check on first division's preparations. Nobel had most of them sweeping the deck and doing other chores. A few manned stations to handle lines. The ten-ton booms were two-blocked. The officer's motor boat, captain's gig, chief-of-staff's gig, and admiral's barge—the four boats under his care—were safely stowed on their individual stands and tied down with guys to the deck. First division stood ready for sea.

72

Flagship

The 1 MC sounded off. "*Bong, bong; bong, bong; bong, bong,* Amphibious Forces Pacific Fleet, arriving, port side." The admiral's car provided by the base, a black Chrysler sporting flags on its front fenders with two stars on a field of blue, pulled to the forward brow. The OOD had the requisite six side boys, all seaman apprentices wearing dress whites, three on either side, and standing at attention on the quarterdeck. The boatswain's mate blew his pipe and the OOD, holding a brass long glass in the crook of his left arm, delivered a smart salute as COMPHIBPAC stepped aboard.

The order exploded over the 1 MC, "Now make all preparations for getting underway," Winthrop's cue. He climbed the ladder to the bridge as the word passed, "Now station the special sea and anchor detail."

Topside, he assumed the watch from the departing quarterdeck OOD and stood by as the ships various departments reported ready for sea to the bridge.

Captain Ridgway welcomed the pilot and soon the boatswain broadcasted, "Now single up all lines fore and aft." Then, "let go all lines, hold the stern line." Winthrop moved to starboard to watch the tug at the bow pull as Eldorado's steam powered the screw pushing from the stern. The vessel would spring out on a single line aft as the force of the tug and the ships engines headed the bow toward the open bay.

When the ship moved to the correct position, the order sounded over the 1 MC, "let go all lines."

Eldorado was underway.

The 1 MC barked, "Underway. Shift colors." Signalmen furled the ensign at the stern and hoisted the colors at the masthead. Pride filled Winthrop as he watched the stars and stripes unfurl overhead.

The boatswain's mate passed the final order on the 1 MC, "Set condition X-ray throughout the ship." As ordered, sailors closed hatches and watertight doors designated "X-ray," spinning the hand wheel or tightening cogs until the gaskets fit snug on their flanges.

Eldorado headed for the combat zone.

~

Going to sea never failed to give Winthrop a high. *Eldorado* wasn't as big as a carrier or a battleship, but she was pretty damn big. As OOD on watch he ran the huge vessel, a machine constructed of steel and other metals but with a life, almost tangible, given to her by the men who served as her crew.

If he screwed up, the court of inquiry would hang him, perhaps a little lower than the captain, but still pretty damn high.

They were going to war. The crew served a role not as close and personal as a Marine or infantryman would, but dangerous nonetheless. Winthrop's heart beat a little faster and he thought of his parents and . . . Mary.

9

Nobel

Nobel's years at sea dealing with officers meant that Winthrop's officiousness the day before didn't bother him. He assumed Winthrop to be smart enough to understand and appreciate him taking charge when he loaded the ship's vehicles without checking first. Nobel chalked up Winthrop's tendency to put on his brass hat now and then as part of the job. Boatswain's Mate First Class Samuel Early Nobel's eighteen years of experience in the Navy taught him to respect officers like Winthrop because the system needed them.

Scared to death of officers as a seventeen-year-old fresh out of boot camp in 1949 where third-class petty officer drill instructors approached the status of God, he matured in the following years. He learned respect for the Navy organizational system. It developed over centuries and dated to the middle ages. Back then aristocrats served as officers, and commoners served as the crew. Today the college education of young officers served a similar purpose as in days of old. A cadre of well-educated men formed a leadership group loyal to each other and the captain. The arrangement maintained discipline and order. The officers weren't demigods, nor were they to be feared. They were men like him trying to do their jobs. And paths were open to sailors like Nobel to advance in their profession or even to jump over to the officer corps.

The order came from the 1 MC. "Single up."

"Single up." Nobel shouted the order to his sailors at the forward lines, leaned over the rail, and repeated the order to the line handlers on the pier.

Back aft, Hoffman, the second division first class duplicated the command to his sailors. Eldorado now floated at the pier attached with six thick hawsers.

A tug stood ready at *Eldorado*'s starboard side with a line over to the ship's bow ready to go. The ship would spring out off a remaining stern line as the forward tug pulled the bow away from the pier.

"Haul in the camels," Nobel ordered.

Sailors pulled up the heavy duty bumpers slung over the side between hull and dock. Mayer, tough for a little guy, got right on the lines. One thing about him Nobel thought, the kid never avoided work like some of the sailors he supervised. Maybe the midnight scrub shower and missing uniform incident straightened him out. Nobel hoped so.

He liked the idea of his division officer leaving him to supervise the forward activities involved in getting underway. *Mister Winthrop, occupied on the bridge, had his own job to do.*

"Hold the stern line. Throw off all other lines," the word came from the phone talker.

"Throw off all forward lines," Nobel shouted. "Hold the tug line."

He felt the rumble as the ship's screw turned and the great bow moved away from the pier.

Moving smartly the second division sailors hauled in the remaining stern line and *Eldorado* moved free of its berth. The tug pulled the bow farther away from the dock and the crew threw off the line. It would come alongside farther out in the channel so the pilot could disembark.

"Underway, shift colors," came the order from the 1 MC.

As the third class petty officers directed the stowing of the ship's lines, Nobel reflected. Not long ago the Navy used manila lines, but now long-lasting nylon replaced the old material. The elasticity of the new stuff gave mooring lines more stretch and created a need to check them more often to make sure they held taut. Nothing ever stayed the same in the Navy. Nobel kept up with the changes. *Don't let yourself slide into incompetence like some old salts I know.*

He walked over to Johnson.

"Better get the port accommodation ladder ready for the pilot," he said.

"Yeah, I got Lee and Mayer on it."

Johnson tended toward cold in dealing with Nobel, but not as bad as with Winthrop. Nobel tried the old fallback. "Get a letter from the old lady? How's the kids?"

"Yeah, she sent pictures. Jerome's on the junior high school basketball team. Shanta's the fifth-grade class secretary."

"Ya must be proud. Never had kids myself. Wish I did."

"Thanks, I got a letter off before we got the word to pull out," Johnson said as he walked away toward the port quarterdeck where Lee and Mayer worked rigging the accommodation ladder.

Damn it was hard to know the guy. He only acted natural around other black sailors.

"Ya gotta show me the pictures." Nobel said to Johnson's back.

As the second-class walked away, his strode loose, his arms like everything about him, long languid, slim. *That's why they call him Slim.*

He carries that damn razor. I can see the cord around his neck, the slight bulge on his back under his uniform.

Nobel tended to be a loner himself but tried to promote fellowship among his men. Good morale pleased him. Johnson mingled with the white sailors enough at the ship's picnic and other division-level stuff, but on his own and on the beach he buddied only with blacks. Nobel didn't like that segregation stuff. He didn't know any black guys growing up, but the natural grouping of sailors with each other along racial lines made him uncomfortable.

Getting to be a regular mother hen, he thought. The brass figured wrong about his alcoholism. Stress on the job didn't cause his former boozing. It was women. If he ever found a woman comfortable with Navy life for dependents, he would be happy. The two he tried to make a life with left him with nothing but scars. A divorce and a nasty breakup with a subsequent girlfriend pushed him into regular drinking. Sure he threw a few benders on the beach in the past, but they weren't serious. It was the women who caused his alcoholism. He loved going to sea. It was his salvation.

~

He married Cheryl, a chick he met in San Diego in 1952. At twenty-one fresh from sea duty and horny as a bull moose in rut, Nobel met her while walking down Broadway.

A freewheeling eighteen-year-old, Cheryl winked at him. He stopped, said, "Hi."

"Hi, back," she said and giggled.

"Are you a native?" he said.

"Are you a real sailor?" she said.

He took her to a club. They lied about her age, drank beer. Cheryl told him she worked as a waitress at a diner on Second Avenue. She wore a pink sweater and bobby socks. She graduated high school the previous June.

He didn't own a car but planned to buy one.

"How can you take me out without a car?" she said.

Flagship

Then, "Do those pants really have thirteen buttons?"

"Where do you live?" he said.

"National City with my parents."

"Long walk?"

"You can take the bus. The same one I take home each day."

That's how it started. In a couple of months, he bought a 1941 Ford. Their restrained necking in her parents' home graduated to heavy petting at the Midway Drive-In. They announced their engagement a week before he shipped out. Her father, a retired chief boilerman, relieved, her mother skeptical, wanted to give them a wedding when he returned from WESTPAC. Instead they married in Tijuana, he resplendent in dress blues, proudly wearing his three decorations: a Combat Action Ribbon, Korean Service Medal, and National Defense Medal, she wearing her mom's gown.

Back then, Nobel recalled, *Eldorado* looked similar as now. As a seaman he had crewed one of the LSTs landing Marines on Red Beach at Inchon, the Navy amphibious landing which flanked the North Koreans and stopped the South from being overrun. Young and eager, he found the opposed landing excited him at first. But he recalled his stark terror when his ship took some hits from North Korean artillery. He survived the battle and earned his third class stripe while aboard. With his promotion, the Navy transferred him to *Eldorado* which arrived after the landing and stayed for four months providing communications and backup flagship duties.

Eldorado returned to San Diego and he met Cheryl.

"Hey, Nobel, stop day dreamin' and come get some coffee," Hoffman, the second division first class, bellowed.

"A minute," Nobel said.

Eldorado headed in the general direction of Grande Island now visible off the starboard bow. The low rumble of the vessel's turbines held steady as she established a course out to sea. She slowed and the tug came alongside to recover the pilot.

Nobel followed Hoffman down to the first class lounge. They poured fresh coffee.

"Don't sweat that CPO crap," Hoffman said. "It'll come buddy."

"Not sweatin' it. Good to get to sea. Gotta check my box."

Nobel didn't want to hear Hoffman try to pump him up. Hoffman meant well but the fucker was too damn solicitous.

Nobel walked over to the deck office, the sea already causing a perceptible rolling motion underfoot. He stood quiet in the deserted space, savoring a minute of solitude.

He picked up the rejected liberty chits to distribute back to his sailors. They knew the score. No liberty, they were going to Vietnam. Too senior to stand watches, Nobel took seriously his position as the top enlisted guy in first division. He poked around, followed up on his men, kept an eye on them for Winthrop, who did stand watches. The Navy worked that way, older experienced officers and enlisted men didn't stand regular watches. Their skills and knowledge remained ready for duty twenty-four hours a day.

And somewhere, under the piled up defenses of experience and rational thought, the emptiness opened in his mind, like the sensation in an express elevator headed down. *Eldorado* wasn't headed on a pleasure cruise, *Eldorado* was headed to war.

~

Next time don't get married in TJ.

Flagship

During Nobel's ten months away at sea, Cheryl found another sailor. They got a marriage license in San Diego and by the time he got back she was long gone, moved to Arkansas or something, he didn't remember. He never officially informed the Navy of his wedding and Eldorado's legal officer advised him TJ marriages were invalid but could cause complications. The officer helped him file some sort of dissolution papers as a precaution in case she ever came after him in later years for some of his retirement, and to clear any records in case he wanted to marry again.

Other than prostitutes, only Cheryl gave him sex in his young life. He succumbed to the fate of too many young sailors, falling for the first chick to give him sex. He never knew what happened to Cheryl. She harbored all the urges of the young also, eager to move out of her parents' home, he guessed, too eager. For all he knew she produced ten kids by now, and Nobel became a footnote in her life. She sure liked to screw, he remembered.

He went out drinking, hitting every bar until they threw him out. The cops picked him up stumbling down Broadway dodging cars, missing one shoe, his hat, and sporting a tattoo of a naked woman on his bare chest. He ended in jail. The Navy busted him back to seaman and transferred him to a LST out of Norfolk.

Lots of females around that place, he thought. Many experienced sex with sailors, few expected to find marriage with them. He adjusted well, worked hard and earned back his third class. He made second class two years later.

He pulled some shore duty at Little Creek and met Nina. Nina Bastos, twenty-nine and divorced, she worked long hours at a commercial laundry. Her two boys, ten and seven attended school near her parents'

81

house. She picked them up after work. The hard labor involved in operating a steam ironing machine kept her body trim, something which first attracted Nobel.

She didn't tell him about the kids until after sleeping with him several times. They used motels because she told him she didn't want her neighbors to talk about her having a man sleep over. By the time she introduced her sons who shared her apartment, she had him hooked.

The arrangement worked for a while, but he felt no bond with her children. She began to talk of marriage.

"Let's wait and see," he said. Her eagerness held him back.

The service assigned him a ship home ported right there in Little Creek, a LSMR. The Navy had converted his unnamed vessel, Landing Ship, Medium, and originally designed for the invasion of Japan, to fire rockets for close support of Marine operating units. The assignment gave him an opportunity to test the relationship. The LSMR went to sea for several months. With his new rank of first-class boatswain's mate he had decided to marry her. When he returned and showed up at her place unannounced he found another man living with her.

The incident sent him off to the nearest barroom. He made the rounds of Little Creek's night clubs ending-up sitting on a curb near the base gate throwing up all over his dress blues and the brand new chevrons of a first class petty officer. That event in the summer of 1958 now lay buried under nine years of living.

In 1962 he earned back his first class and stayed out of bars and avoided the women who inhabited them. Now at thirty-six years old and committed to a Navy career, his assignment to *Eldorado* seemed a good omen for his chances of getting the CPO rank. Now the promotion may not happen, but he was at sea again. He decided to gut it out. Maybe he could make chief yet, but even without the advancement he held a good job, enjoyed great chow, a place to sleep, and a retirement plan. He figured the war would go on for a few years, so the cutbacks that always came after a conflict wouldn't hit for some time, long enough for him to make his twenty. If necessary he could retire at age thirty-eight. Not like many of his classmates who finished high school and got themselves lost in hometown jobs. Not many ways to make a living in his birthplace, Caribou, Maine.

10

Johnson

"Wrap it up Lee," Johnson said. "Okay, good work, Mayer."

J. J. the Man as the kids in Detroit called him. He and Downtown Charlie Brown cut slick figures leanin' while cruisin' in the old yellow Chrysler on Saturday nights.

As the seamen two-blocked the accommodation ladder he recalled the convertible he and Charlie bought in a junkyard and repaired enough to drive. "Leanin'," Mister Winthrop didn't know what to say when J. J. described the practice to him on one quiet watch crossing the Pacific. He didn't talk much to officers, not wanting to give them anything to use to manipulate him. *That was it. Those white boy officers always try to manipulate us brothers. Gotta guard against that. Cool, J.J., cool.*

He told Winthrop that to "lean" you sat way back in the car's seat, one hand on the wheel, with a slick hat low over your eyes and the other arm laid out comfortable-like along the edge of the door and drivin' down the main road on a Saturday night. He and Downtown Brown did a lot of crusin', a lot, till he met Leticia. She put a stop to it.

Now a days, his old pal Charlie Brown squandered his life away in prison. *Thank God for Leticia. That chick got his slim frame into church, made him enlist. Now look at me. Here I am ordering white boys around.*

"Y'all startin' ta act like a real sailor, Mayer. Gonna tell Mister Winthrop ya Ok." Feeling cocky, he laid on the black Southern lingo. *Damn I can be cool.* Jerome no-middle-name Johnson one of three sons born to a God-fearing family in the Brewster Projects climbed out of the ghetto with the help of a good wife and the Navy.

He directed his attention to Lee. "Y'all hear anything from Reilly?"

"Naw, I heard he's picked Sully in second division."

"That bastard went and recruited Sully after I told him you wanted the job." Johnson's old temper raged, a temper which almost put him in jail once. He swallowed the emotion, thought of his kids . . . and Leticia.

"I spoke to Winthrop about it, but he's another white guy. Not many brothers in the officer corps."

It was Leticia who convinced him a better life existed outside the projects if he enlisted in the Navy. She kept him cool in a certain way, but Johnson carried something else, a confidence maker. Some of the white sailors wore crosses under their uniforms. Not J.J. He hid a blade, a folded straight-edge razor, slim like himself, and deadly, worn in a soft leather sheath hung on a leather shoelace, around his neck, not on his chest but low on his back, under his uniform, something he could reach at any time.

He had not used it yet. He pulled it once on the beach. The other guy backed off. Not like the projects, sailors didn't sneak up on ya aboard ship, but the blade made him feel safe, confident. He needed a razor back then, always. *Too many thugs and addicts in those high rises*. Buildings for the poor, they called them. He didn't know how his old man made it working a "city job." City job, ha. He worked as a fuckin' janitor. Slim was gonna do better. The other black sailors started calling him Slim in the PBRs. He liked the nickname, cooler than J.J., mysterious, tough. "Watch out for Slim," they'd say.

No one challenged him. The black guys, even the white guys, different in the Navy. Sailors, not thugs, they "had your back." Ya didn't have to "watch your back," not like in the projects. Shipmates cover for ya on the beach. If some sailor off another ship picked a fight ya could count on your shipmates. He fought in a few brawls. They were more ship versus ship or squibs versus grunts, never shipmates against each other. *Hell, I'm getting to be a "Navy man," a damn old salt.*

Still, he felt more comfortable with black buddies, but he started to notice the white sailors weren't the bastards they called whites in the projects. *What about Winthrop? Would he help? Winthrop's too fucking detached to help.*

The 1 MC squawked, rousing him out of his thoughts, "Set condition X-ray throughout the ship." He headed below to check on his spaces, make sure the assigned sailors closed the X-ray hatches.

Hell, he thought, going to 'Nam on this ship ain't much, no worries about fire-fights like in the PBRs. No sweatin' like a pig working on the rivers lookin' for Charlie behind every vine, every tree, sometimes finding a kid with an old gun, just a kid, but a deadly kid. His crew stopped every Vietnamese boat it ran into and searched it. Caught some contraband, but most were just local fishermen. The days ran long, hot, boring. A few times the days got deadly. Those deadly days woke him nights with dreams he hated, but earned him a Combat Action Ribbon.

Back in the states, before his ship deployed he took the family to see *Sand Pebbles,* a movie that defined for all time the American sailor in the old China fleet. Few in 1966 San Diego ever heard of those days in the Navy before watching the movie. Funny, how Hollywood made it real, sort of. Johnson was smart enough to know reality from Hollywood. The real life in a gunboat, he figured, ran gamier and grubbier and the real glory ran tainted by folly.

"Daddy," Shanta had said, "how come there aren't any black people in the movie?

"Don't know," he had said. "Maybe there weren't any of us dumb enough to join the Navy in those days."

Because the China fleet had all those Chinese coolies, they didn't need us to do the servant work.

Shanta will learn someday.

The deep rumble of *Eldorado*'s engine called him back. On bridge watches he held sway as senior enlisted man on deck regardless of any sailor's rank. Boatswain's mate of the watch, an important responsibility not like "leanin,'" back home. On the ship real people depended on him even the white watch officers. A train of goose flesh ran up his back beneath his "confidence" razor. *This ain't crusin' the boulevard.*

His thoughts turned to Leticia and the kids.

11

Mayer

Seaman Mayer, son of Normandy hero and MIA Private Earnest Royal Mayer, hauled on the line hoisting the accommodation ladder. A green island glimmering off the starboard bow steered his thoughts to topless dancing girls in grass skirts.

His new buddy Zack Lee grasped the line with him and with his ever-present grin said, "Ain't that Grande Island over there? Hear they throw picnics and parties on it. Guess we ain't gonna get there on this trip."

They secured the ladder to the ship's side, removed and stowed the block and tackle arrangement, and headed below to drink some coffee on the mess deck.

"You got the twelve to four?" Mayer said.

"Yeah, I got the port lookout."

"Winthrop pulled me off messenger duty. Johnson still training you to replace me?"

"Yeah, he don't like Winthrop either."

Mayer recalled Winthrop's ordered meeting with the chaplain. *He didn't like it. Turned out okay.* The chaplain arranged to replace his stolen uniforms and urged him to write to his mother.

"Sometimes talking to someone you trust, helps," he had said.

Thus Mayer agreed to meet with the chaplain once a week. He knew the guy was trying to get him to accept Jesus, but he enjoyed the talks. So he ignored the man's efforts at religious promotion and continued to meet with him.

Flagship

Mayer never attended church. His mother rejected all religion; said God didn't help her after his old man went missing at Normandy. *Missing, ha, the Army still said he was missing. Woulda turned up by now. He was dead, stone-cold dead.*

Mayer knew his old man worked in ship construction, and his mother told him the name of the last ship he worked on, the S S *Monsoon*, which the Navy renamed *Eldorado* and turned into a command ship. He told no one about his old man building *Eldorado*; just about him probably dying at Normandy.

The chaplain got him new uniforms. Couldn't knock that, but Winthrop, he wasn't sure.

"Mister Winthrop, why?"

"Winthrop only assigns him black boys to train."

"Winthrop didn't do nothin' to help me when someone stole my uniforms."

He knew that wasn't true. The officer sent him to see the chaplain. *So I swiped some change when I was messenger, I needed it more than they did.*

"Those officers don't care about us."

He realized that wasn't true either.

Lee had heard some of the guys saying Mayer was a sneak thief. The guy never stole from him.

"He sent me to the chaplain," Mayer went on, "an' I think he ordered the scrub shower."

"Scrub shower?"

"Before you came aboard. It was, was hazing."

Mayer struggled to control emotions he didn't understand. Frustration, hatred, and self-pity ran through his head. Life never treated him right.

"He don't care 'bout po' folk like us, Lee said. Won't help me break into the print shop. But Johnson got an idea 'bout that. What da ya put in your coffee?" He grabbed the pot.

"Drink it black," Mayer said.

They maneuvered around other sailors and found an empty spot on one of the steel tables and hunkered down with their cups.

The 1 MC squawked, "Secure the special sea and anchor detail. Set the normal underway watch."

Lee paused, mid sip.

"We goin' to the combat zone," he said.

"When do we get to a port?" Mayer said.

"Not sure. Bode says we stay at sea thirty or forty days. We anchor sometimes but no liberty."

"They shoot at us?"

"Sometimes, not sure. Bode says we earn R and R every couple of months," Lee grinned. "He says them chicks in Bangkok make you forget Vietnam. Better than Olongapo girls."

12

Steve Taylor relieved Winthrop at 0945 when the captain secured the sea and anchor detail. Winthrop signed his log and walked down several levels to the deck office to handle any administrative work backed up in his basket. He planed to eat lunch before assuming the watch once again at noon. The one-in-three rotation for the combat zone had started.

Trucker, at his desk, puffing a cigarette, turned and greeted him as he removed his overseas hat and sat.

"Those piss-cutters are okay in the tropics, less sweat, but they fuckin' wilt easy."

"Mine's already floppy," Winthrop said fingering the flat little hat worn at sea in the tropics. He reached for his cigarette pack, decided against smoking, instead putting the Winston's in his shirt pocket.

"Supply officer spoke to me about some buzz on the mess decks," Trucker said. "Thinks Johnson started it. Wondered why."

"What's that?"

Trucker leaned back in his chair.

"The print shop never sends anyone mess cooking because they only got petty officers. Ain't fair they say. Lot of the deck guys are grumbling."

"Johnson wants Reilly to pick Lee as his new striker," Winthrop said. "Maybe something to do with that. Word is Reilly wants Sully from second division."

Randolph slid his chair around across the compartment, faced them, "Sully's pissed because he just finished his three months as a mess

91

cook, took his turn. Now he'll get assigned again if he strikes for lithographer's mate."

"Yeah, nobody likes that job." Winthrop said.

Like all US ships *Eldorado* employed specialist cooks and supplemented them with unrated sailors to do the manual labor involved in serving 450 men in the ships company and the 50 men on the admiral's staff three meals a day. The sailors were conscripted from other departments and worked three-month tours.

"He's a rough kid to begin with. now he's bitching about mess cooking all the time," Randolph said. "Says one mess cooking term is enough for a four-year enlistment."

"Well, you know how the XO is about morale," Trucker said. "A little grumbling from the crew is normal, even good, shows they are being pushed about right, but if it gets outta hand . . ."

"Christ," Winthrop said, "Johnson again."

"Can't solve that problem now." Trucker took his hat. "Wonder what rice concoction the stewards got for us today."

~

Winthrop piled his plate with rice, then heaped on the meat, mushrooms, and gravy, took a sip of water. The rice would expand in his stomach, make him bloated on watch, uncomfortable, but what-the-hell he thought. *Ya only live once, Winthrop.*

"Reilly in the print shop, he's pissed as hell," Larsen said, looking at Winthrop. "Heard he's gotta send someone mess cooking."

"Word travels fast," Winthrop said. "It's just a rumor."

"Oh yeah? Larsen waved a glass of milk. Look at the head table. Edger and the supply officer got their heads together with the XO. It's about the mess cookin' detail."

92

"Wonder if they know the whole story. Look at that hapless grin on Edger's face. He's tryin' to figure out what the XO wants so he can agree with it."

"Hey, Edger's my boss," Larsen said with a chuckle.

"So how you gonna handle Reilly if Edger says you gotta sent the striker mess cookin'?" Chips asked Ensign Larsen.

"I'll just tell him Lieutenant Commander Edger ordered it."

"No, you gotta tell him *you* are ordering it. He will respect you then. If you don't, Reilly will go to Edger and Edger will be pissed at you for not doin' your job."

"Chips is right, Harley," Winthrop said, "You're the boss. *You* give the order. It's your job. Anyway, I worked with Reilly. You give him that opening; he'll ask Edger and forever go around you to him. Didn't ya learn anything at OCS?"

Winthrop pulled out the pack of Winstons and his Zippo. He lit up, pushed his plate away, and reached for the coffee pot. *Shit, smoking again.*

"I know how to run my division," Larsen said, "but I gotta back up my first-class."

Chandler, the W-4 warrant officer, shook his head. "Well Chipper, old pal, makes you wonder about these college boy ensigns, how the Navy survives 'em."

Chips chuckled.

"I'll tell you what I did when my first-class refused to send a man for pier sentry duty," Dunston said. "He claimed his guys had too much to do. Ordered *him* to sentry duty. He decided right on the spot to send a seaman."

"Ya see, Mister Larsen," Chips said, "now that's how you make JG."

"Aww, it's automatic." He folded his skinny arms.

"Don't count on it, Larsen," Winthrop said. "Gotta go on watch now." He pulled his chair out, downed his coffee and headed for the bridge. Dunston followed.

~

In the evening, he ate dinner during the short break provided by the dog watches. Then Winthrop trudged up weather deck ladders and assumed the conn on the bridge for the eight to twelve.

He sipped on a strong cup of quartermaster coffee, and grimaced. The navigators, called quartermasters in the Navy, kept a pot brewing in their shop located behind the wheel house. The forty-cup coffee maker produced great stuff, but as hours wore on and the water steamed away the java tended toward bitter. Winthrop took his bridge watch coffee black, simpler that way. He lit a cigarette, walked out to the starboard wing of the bridge and stood next to Dunston.

"Quiet night," he said.

Dunston scanned the sky ahead.

"Yeah, see those lights tracking near the big dipper—a commercial airplane probably. How 'bout we ask CIC to check if they are squawking, wake 'em up down there."

"Go for it."

All aircraft operated a transceiver which responded to radar sweeps with an Identification, Friend or Foe code, called IFF. The device produced a simple series of lines on the radar screen showing the aircraft to be a friendly. Lack of such a code emanating from a blip on the air search radar didn't prove hostile intent but would be cause for concern.

Dunston walked over to the 1 MC, flicked the lever.

"Combat, Bridge, is that aircraft squawking?"

"What aircraft?"

"Stop the game of hearts and check the air search radar. Put it on IFF mode for Christ's sake."

"Huh, Combat, aye."

Winthrop shook his head.

~

Eldorado continued to Da Nang harbor, arrived February 8 and anchored. From the flagship's vantage the harbor could be anywhere in the tropical world. The view included other ships moored here and there, a pier in the distance, some non-descript buildings and greenery. Eldorado's boats not in current use road quietly in the water, held by sea painters attached to the ship's port boat boom. An accommodation ladder leading to the quarterdeck handled incoming and departing boat passengers.

The one-in-three watch rotation continued with no liberty allowed for the crew. The old "hurry-up-and-wait" adage of the military applied. After the urgent departure from Subic, the ship stayed anchored for several days, the crew sitting tight. Security conditions required the setting of armed sentries, the rigging of waterline lights and stationing an armed picket boat which circled the ship. Winthrop and Dunston each carried an Ithaca .45 pistol while on watch. The weapons were passed on, watch to watch. The admiral and his staff attended meetings on the beach and officials came and went, some by boat, some by chopper. The second division flight deck guys were active.

Winthrop found his natural rhythm disrupted because the dog watches broke the rotation so no one stood the same watch the same time each day, producing a sort of zombie effect on the consciousness. He spent his time standing watch, eating, sleeping and, when he could, visiting the deck office to do paperwork. The days blended.

13

On February 14 *Eldorado* weighed anchor and set course to an Amphibious Objective Area off Quang Ngai Provence, south of Da Nang.

Winthrop woke from deep sleep as the twelfth "bong" of the thirteen sounded for Battle Stations. Shaking his head clear he heard the 1 MC: "This is not a drill, this is not a drill. General quarters, General quarters. All hands man your battle stations. Bong, bong . . ." He pulled on his pants pushed his arms into his shirt sleeves, pulled on his socks and shoes, grabbed his helmet out of his locker and headed for the bridge while tucking in his shirt. Operation Deckhouse VI, a Marine landing by the Special Landing Force had commenced.

He ran forward on the starboard side as men rushed through officer country toward their battle stations. The convention, forward on the starboard, aft on the port side, kept the stampede orderly.

The 1 MC announced "Set condition Zulu throughout the ship"

He took stock on the bridge, his battle station, junior officer of the deck, an indicator of the old man's esteem. But a more experienced officer, LT Joe Trucker took over as officer of the deck for general quarters. Winthrop was an extra hand, no specific assignment, just standby for anything. Through the mist of the early dawn he spotted two smaller vessels, LSMRs, rocket ships, close to shore. They fired broadsides inland.

Engineering, checking in on the 21 MC, reported the ship's watertight doors buttoned up with condition Zulu set in all compartments.

Trucker approached him.

"Fred, how about taking the radio hand set and reporting our fixes to the flag? The quartermaster's calling them out. The captain has the conn."

The departments reported in over the 21 MC intercom: "combat, manned and ready, damage control, manned and ready, gun control, manned and ready . . ." A sailor checked them off on a status board.

Winthrop picked up the radiotelephone hand set on the forward bulkhead already set to the correct channel by a guy from com. After a radio check, he started reporting using the ship's call sign as the quartermaster called out the fix.

"This is Decanter Tango, 500 yards from anchorage."

Standing forward in the wheelhouse he viewed the battle scene as it unfolded. Several waves of choppers passed over head as Marines headed for their landing zones. The concept of vertical envelopment involved landing marines by chopper inland a few miles, the plan being to catch the enemy between them and the Marines hitting the beach. Winthrop spotted a wave of Amtraks, tank-like armored landing craft, churning toward the shore, followed by two or three waves of World War II style landing boats designated LCVPs and called papa boats.

Marines, *God bless the Marines*, Winthrop thought. Some of them would die today. Young men from villages and towns and cities all over the United States, enough of them to mount a real fighting force. Despite the demonstrations and the flood of draft dodgers headed for Canada, the nation still produced young men of honor.

They faced everything from the NVA and Viet Cong bullets and punji sticks, to malaria, heat strokes, and poisonous snakes. They would be in country for days, maybe get a drink from a canteen and a MRE, "meal-ready-to-eat," if they were lucky, wolfed down in a fox hole.

Winthrop could stroll down to the wardroom and pour himself a cup of coffee after the landing while the grunts would suffer depravation and danger for days.

Everyone has a role to play, Winthrop. Do your job. It's the best way to help them.

"This is Decanter Tango, 300 yards from anchorage," he said.

A few minutes later he heard the captain.

"Drop the hook."

One of his first division guys swung a sledge and hit a stay on the pelican hook restraining the anchor. The chain thundered from its locker forming a torrent out the hawse. *Eldorado's* now creeping movement pulled the hook deep into the sand under the South China Sea.

"Decanter Tango, anchored," Winthrop reported. Somewhere up on the flag bridge a sailor marked it on a status board showing the whole scene in miniature for the admiral.

Helmeted sailors manned *Eldorado's* guns, the old five-inch thirty-eight mounted on the bow, capable of throwing a five-inch shell five miles, and the lethal twin forty-millimeter mounts on either side of the forward boat deck. In gun control, Winthrop's buddy, Jay Dunston stood as gunnery officer ready to put the ancient weapons to use in the unlikely event they were needed. But *Kitty Hawk*, just over the horizon, could send F-4 phantoms with air support if the cruiser with its modern guns patrolling offshore couldn't do the job.

The old man hung up the bridge phone near the chart table.

"Flight quarters." He said to Nobel, serving as boatswains mate for general quarters.

Nobel blew his pipe and announced; "Flight quarters, flight quarters."

An incoming Huey headed toward the flagship.

Winthrop moved aft along the bridge deck to overlook the landing platform on the stern. Two sturdy stanchions, festooned with antennas, rose forty feet directly in front of the helicopter landing deck. They blocked the forward three-quarters of the ship from the choppers setting down, requiring them to approach from either quarter. In that way they could slip off to the opposite side without hitting one of the antenna supports. Landing from dead astern presented a dangerous lack of an escape route in an emergency.

The chopper landed without incident, disgorging a young marine officer with a satchel of messages direct for the admiral. The flight quarters crew secured the craft as its rotors slowed. A grim Marine crouched with a machine gun at the open gun bay of the Huey.

Winthrop walked back to the bridge as the announcement came: "Secure from general quarters. Set condition X-ray." His wristwatch read 6:45. *An hour and a quarter for breakfast before my watch.*

~

Eldorado weighed anchor at dusk and got underway, steaming back and forth in the area. She would spent nine days lingering in the locale, most of her crew working the one-in-three duty schedule so that nearly one-third of the crew stood watch at any time. Routine work came to a stop. An "open racks" policy prevailed. Crewmen slept anytime they had a chance. Winthrop and the other junior officers began calling the ship the admiral's taxi, their knowledge of the marine operation limited to what they gleaned from the OOD's message clipboard, which they were expected to read on each watch. The crew knew less, and doggedly went about their jobs. Boredom and fatigue prevailed.

Talk in the wardroom became subdued—eat, work, and go find your rack or watch station, the rule. Continued maneuvering, attention to other ships and contacts in the area, identifying them, avoiding them, and supervising the watch, not just on the bridge, but the whole third of the crew on duty, drained Winthrop's energy. Still, he managed to follow his orders without faltering. Recovery of his sharpness before each upcoming watch took longer as the days passed. Par for the course, Winthrop figured. *The Marines had it worse.*

The hospital ship, *Sanctuary,* had arrived on the scene on day one. Choppers flying back and forth from the beach to the white ship's helo platform carried casualties, Marines with everything from heat stroke to gut wounds received the best treatment their country could provide, the horrendous losses the US suffered in Vietnam lessened by on-the-scene medical attention.

~

Eldorado's old five-inch, thirty-eight, bow gun loomed in the darkness in front of Winthrop, beyond the boat deck and ten-ton booms. *I'll be twenty-four in a couple of months, and here I am an old salt standing a bridge watch in the combat zone.*

In the depth of his fatigue was the fear; was he up to it tonight? He seemed to exist on coffee and cigarettes these days. The great carrier, *Kitty Hawk,* moved like a shadow, through the golden river of moonlight off the flagship's starboard side and seemed to merge with it. Fred Winthrop shook himself.

Shit, I guess it's possible to fall asleep standing up.

Winthrop lit a cigarette and hoped the starboard lookout hadn't seen him doze off.

He stepped back into the pilothouse and nodded at Johnson, whose boatswain's pipe hung from his neck on an immaculately white lanyard. In a languid stance near the weather deck hatch, his pursed lips revealed his tension.

"Quiet night," Winthrop said.

Eyes lidded, Johnson said, "Yes sir." The words came out unsteady, not casual and cold, his normal reaction to Winthrop.

Nodding, keeping up his image, Winthrop said, "Yea, hard to stay awake." *I'm shaky as him.*

He took a drag on the cigarette.

In front of him, Dunston stood hunched over a radar repeater. Winthrop poked him with his elbow.

"Wake-up, Dunston."

He jumped, then grinned. "Wasn't dozing, Fred, just marking contacts on the radar. That big blip is *Kitty Hawk*"

Winthrop moved across the centerline, past the helmsman, and stuffed out his smoke in the old shell casing on the chart table. His mind went back to the quiet night in his sophomore year on the roof of the apartment building in Boston. The moon then looked the same as tonight's. The roof overlooked Commonwealth Avenue. He, his roommates, and some girls from another apartment were up there drinking beer at the end of the summer. One of the girls sure was hot for him.

His head dropped and he jerked it up. *Oops*, he thought, *Wake-up Winthrop.* He lit another cigarette.

Flagship

He looked around to get his head clear, still on the bridge, thoughts drifted again back to the girl. She had clung to him immediately after that night. He hadn't wanted a serious relationship; after all, he still had his youth, couldn't even remember her name now. She came back in some of his dreams. He forced his mind to Mary and sighed. He really needed some liberty. He looked through the wheelhouse porthole toward the bow at the clear night sky—thoughts tumbling around.

When we get some R&R, I'll sleep for two days before I go on the beach.

Then his mind drifted to the delights of Asian women. He shook his head again, took another drag, thought of Mary.

Winthrop's feet hurt. The one-in-three watch rotation offered no chance of relief. Just when the numb throbbing of his legs started easing from the previous watch, he stood on the bridge again, the same sensation of steel-hard pain running right up into his shins. He looked dully at his Corfam brown shoes.

I still got three hours of this shit. I need another cup of coffee.

Flares glowed on the beach to port. The Marines engaged a vaporous foe. At least up north most of the enemy consisted of regular soldiers, not the children the Viet Cong often used in the south. The North Vietnamese army used flares. Probably some poor marine caught out in the open, he thought. He took another drag. The cigarette glowed red, nearing the filter. He stubbed it out and lit another. His thoughts provoked his anger, waking him a bit, as he remembered the outcries from the antiwar peaceniks when General Curtis Lemay famously suggested the US bomb North Vietnam back to the Stone Age.

His wash khaki uniform showed the underarm salt stains from the day before, and dark moisture destined to create more salt stains.

103

Might as well forget the niceties of deodorant in this place, he thought. His piss-cutter hat lost the crisp sharp top of the earlier, morning watch. The little shield and anchor device pinned to the left side dangled precipitously. *He'd dig a fresh one out of his drawer after breakfast.* His gonads itched like crazy under pants hanging like limp drapes on aching legs.

Earlier, after the dogwatch, he had gone straight to the wardroom for dinner. He should have hit the rack then, but feeling shaky from all the coffee he took in the wardroom movie. Later, he walked to his stateroom to sleep.

Winthrop had climbed into his bunk at 2200 hours. Dead tired, he skipped a shower and simply lay in the rack in his T-shirt and khaki pants. Still, he tossed and turned far too long before falling asleep. The messenger of the watch had shaken him awake at 0345.

Now, he glanced at his wrist.

Fuck, only five o'clock. How could he stay awake until 0800, he mumbled? He headed for the quartermaster shack just aft of the pilothouse. Full of charts, the navigation guys hung out there.

Tripping as he stepped through the hatch into the dimly lit compartment he encountered a single small red light bulb glowing in the corner near the coffee pot. It'll taste like bilge oil, Winthrop thought, unless someone made a fresh pot. The stuff trickled out of the spigot—the bottom dredges.

"Hey, Hertzberg, how about breaking down and making a new pot," he said to the duty quartermaster.

Winthrop had the captain's night orders memorized. *Continue in the night steaming area maneuvering as required until further notice.* He reviewed the rules of engagement in his mind. There seemed little likelihood tonight the ship would have to fight off an attack. His fatigue swelled in him again and his vision turned fuzzy. The pit of fear tightened in his stomach. He took a sip of the strong coffee.

As Winthrop dragged himself back to the bridge, Dunston shouted, "Hey, Fred, need you starboard."

Hustling to the starboard wing of the bridge, he found Dunston pointing and standing near the lookout.

"Crap, must have incoming wounded," Winthrop said.

The massive hospital ship loomed close on a steady bearing. Ignoring the rules of the road, she had turned into the old flagship's path creating a possible collision if someone didn't maneuver.

Extremis, the point when the projected track of two ships would result in a collision unless both ships maneuvered, loomed near, perhaps two minutes away. The existing aspects of the two ships burdened the flagship. *Eldorado* must maneuver and the hospital ship must maintain course and speed.

The hospital ship often broke the rules like that, no call on the radio, no warning at all, just assuming other ships would avoid her, and the brass tolerated such actions. Supposedly, she turned to get some extra relative wind coming over her flight deck in order to ease the landing of choppers. No wind existed on the flat calm sea this night. The relative wind came from the bow no matter what course the ship chose.

His mouth dry, Winthrop turned abruptly toward the pilothouse. "Left full rudder," he ordered. *Fuck,* he thought.

Johnson, jaw clenched, moved behind the junior seaman at the helm, showing why Winthrop liked him on the bridge. He would take the large wheel if the helmsman choked, but the kid responded as trained.

He sung out. "Aye, aye sir, left full rudder."

105

Then, "Rudder is left full, sir."

Following protocol, Winthrop responded, "Very well, continue left to course one nine zero." Inside his heart pounded–*don't show it,* he thought, as the rudder delay on the huge ship kept her on course for a seeming indeterminable interval.

Finally, the reliable old girl groaned, shuttered, and started to turn to port. Fully awake now, Winthrop put his binoculars on the hospital ship, dropping the cigarette. The adrenalin flooded his system. He closed his eyes for a moment, consciously slowing his breathing.

He turned to Dunston.

"Thanks for the heads up buddy," he said. "Christ, a bunch of fuckin' doctors must be running that ship instead of sailors."

Already off to starboard as *Eldorado* came about to port, the white hospital ship looked like a pale ghost in the moonlight as a little black shape in the sky approached her helo deck. The shape became a chopper. The craft landed with a desperate urgency.

Winthrop eyed the chopper. *Wounded*, he thought, and a picture of a Marine with a sucking chest wound flashed into his mind. His breathing under control now, he sighed, picked up the cigarette and spoke to Dunston.

"Jay, go ahead and take the conn," he said.

I can hack the rest of this watch. Winthrop headed back to the quartermaster shack for more coffee. The fresh brew smelled invigorating.

~

Eldorado left the area a few days early, sailed to Okinawa, and anchored in Buckner Bay for a four-day stop over from February 24 to February 28. The crew got liberty.

106

Flagship

Phase 1 of Deckhouse VI ended February 26 with 201 enemy kills claimed at the expense of six Marines dead. The landing force captured twenty tons of enemy supplies and claimed 167 fortifications destroyed. Phase II started February 27 without *Eldorado.*

14

Winthrop slept for twelve hours, waking on time for breakfast on Saturday, February 25. He took extra time enjoying a hot shower. He shaved more carefully than usual, taking his time with the lather and the Gillett razor. Naha would be the destination in the evening.

Okinawa hosted several US bases, a result of treaties with Japan after the war. The Okinawans viewed the US as liberators and welcomed Americans but the economy, boosted by the greenbacks flowing out of pockets of serviceman stationed there gave the women good paying jobs. Prostitution was limited. Bar girls only hustled drinks for the most part. With Mary on his mind Winthrop wouldn't chase the local girls anyway, but hoped to enjoy a good meal and a few drinks with the guys.

At officer's call, he learned he drew shore patrol duty for that evening. No carousing on Saturday night for him. No chance to get in trouble. *Good, keep me out of trouble with Mary.*

~

Nobel

Nobel; Marty Hoffman, the first class in second division; Elam Jones, a gunner's mate first class; and a couple of chiefs from engineering took the liberty boat to the White Beach pier at Buckner Bay. They rented a cab outside the gate and asked the driver to take them to a good restaurant in Naha.

Called The Snake's Breath Tavern, the place included a nightclub and an attached restaurant. The nightclub featured Habushu, music, bar girls, and one or two scantily clad prostitutes scattered about. The restaurant offered Kobe beef steaks which they all ordered.

Nobel passed on a glass of Habushu sake from a bottle which included a rice wine-embalmed dead Habu snake. He ordered a Sapporo instead. When the beer arrived he took a sip and listened quietly to the conversation. From across the room the men could hear a Japanese vocalist singing on a stage backed by a three-man rock band. In her short-shorts, and a tight-fitting, low cut top, she pranced around on high-heeled white boots. Diminutive in size, but with a big voice, she warbled out *These Boots Are Made for Walkin'* in a voice better than Nancy Sinatra's—softer, more lady-like, Nobel decided.

Some of the deck guys sat around the band area drinking beer. Nobel recognized Lee, the kid from first division, dancing with one of the bar girls. Always a showman, Lee put on an exaggerated interpretation of the song to the cheers of the patrons.

Sullivan didn't cheer. He stared at Mayer, sitting with Lee's friends—some other black sailors.

Nobel spotted him, poked Hoffman. "Keep an eye on your man Sullivan. There's gonna be trouble."

Sailors off the USS *Bayfield* sat nearby and cheered the same scene. Most were black. They clapped for Lee's moves. Lee bounced around on the floor as the bar girl pretended to walk all over him.

Sullivan got out of his chair, tried to cut in. The girl shunned him. He stood swaying, crocked. Short, but solid with a pug nose, blond hair clipped tight, Sullivan slurred his words. "What makes you think you can showoff, boy?"

The music stopped, Lee started to get up. Mayer rose to help his buddy, hesitated, and then shoved Sullivan away.

109

"He da one wants da print shop," Lee said.

"What you doin', Sully? Mayer said, "We're having fun. Go sit down."

Two *Bayfield* sailors came over.

They spoke to Lee. "Trouble, brother?"

Nobel shook his head, nodded at the guys at his table. "We better break this up."

The five approached the dance floor, three first class petty officers, two chiefs, all wearing their service dress whites.

The *Bayfield* sailors spotted their ship patches, USS *Eldorado*.

"We'll handle this, fellas," Nobel said, addressing the *Bayfield* guys.

One, a third class, considered Nobel through lidded eyes, reminding Nobel of Johnson's habitual stare when addressing senior white guys. "We stick up for a brother."

"This is an *Eldorado* thing" Nobel said. "Go stick up for your own crewmen."

Lee stood next to Mayer.

"I got his back," Mayer said.

~

Johnson

Johnson sat in the corner of The Snake's Breath Tavern restaurant eating Kobe beef with a couple of guys from supply. His wife Leticia's, influence kept him from interfering with Lee and the *Bayfield* sailors. *Jerome, she had said, think of me and the kids when you gonna do somethin' stupid.*

Mayer, *Weasel*, he thought, stood up for Lee. What's a white boy doin' with black boys, he wondered? Since the guys swiped all his uniforms and the chaplain bought him new ones Mayer's more sociable, mostly with Lee but maybe he learned something. That Sullivan is strong. A short bastard, but strong, Lee don't need a run in with him, lose his chance at the print shop by fighting. Maybe I can get Mayer to fight for him.

He watched the *Bayfield* sailors return to their table. The dance floor gleamed in scattered places with the waxy shine left by the cleaning crew of the early morning. Distinct smudges from the shoe soles of men who treaded in untold places before entering the night spot disrupted the luster. Johnson reflected upon the immortal souls of those same men. Sullivan, he understood. Johnson *knew* white men hated black men. That he knew. What he didn't know was why Mayer stood up for Lee. His questions grew, not just about Mayer, but about Nobel and other sailors who tried to befriend him, even officers like Winthrop. Johnson reached to his back, felt the comforting thin, sharp straight edge in its sheath resting at the small of his back.

The band started up and the singer launched into *When a Man Loves a Woman.* Sailors grabbed bar girls to dance, and the Sullivan incident faded.

~

Mayer

Mayer and Lee sat at their table. A bar girl joined them. Mayer bought her a drink.

"Put it on a tab," she said, reaching out and touching him under the table.

Mayer looked at Lee, back at the girl.

"This Japanese girl like you," she said.

"Japanese? This is Okinawa."

111

"I'm from Yokohama. This is my cousin's place."

"Better pay now, probably expensive," Lee said. "This ain't Olongapo."

"No tab," Mayer said.

The girl got up, "Twenty dollar, please."

Lee tasted her drink, "Crap, 'twenty dollar.' It's tea."

"Pay-up," the girl persisted.

"Here's a buck. Get lost," Mayer said.

A sailor from *Bayfield* strolled over. "You like me better?" He strutted for the bar girl.

She looked at his sleeve. The two chevrons marked him as a second class.

"You big spender?"

"Ya, babe," the *Bayfield* guy said.

They walked away.

15

At breakfast the next day Winthrop told his table about his shore patrol duty the night before.

"So the liberty boat was late and I'm standing above the pier with a couple of enlisted guys. You know how it is. They tell you to call the base hard hats with any problems. We sorta show the flag with our SP arm bands.

"So the boat's still not there and the sailors start piling up down on the pier drunk and getting rowdy. All we got for weapons is the damn phone."

"Don't they train you or anything?" Larsen said.

'No, it's kinda like when *Eldorado* visits a foreign port. Our guns make us a man-of-war, but we couldn't shoot our way out of a modern attack. Just the fact that we are around keeps the seas open. It's a perception thing. They think we have power. Therefore we do have power."

Winthrop took a sip of coffee, lit a cigarette. "That only works so well. I found out last night. I told my crew I'd go down there and calm the rowdies down. Must have been fifty of 'em."

"Lucky they didn't throw your ass in the drink," Chips said.

"Yeah, they yelled 'Where's the fuckin' liberty boat.' Then they started sayin' 'Throw his ass in the water.' They were all drunk."

"So what happened?" Larsen said. Winthrop could see Larsen was hoping he screwed up.

"I got the fuck outta there. Lucky the boat showed a few minutes later."

113

"Ya did the right thing." Chips said. "If they had thrown you in, some might have got themselves kicked out of the Navy. The brass would back you up but they wouldn't like it. They don't want to lose good sailors over a drunken incident like that."

Merlin Chandler, the other warrant officer at the table weighed in. "You know you junior officers provide a great service to the Navy standing shore patrol. You give just about every veteran who served a great story for the grandkids about running from the shore patrol."

The others chuckled, sensed a sage bit of lore coming from the old salt.

"Have you ever heard of a shore patrol actually catching a sailor?" The wry grin revealed the obvious. The answer was no. But there were plenty of examples of sailors who escaped.

"Naw," Chandler said, "the brass don't expect ya too. It's all for show. It meets DOD requirements but the professional hard hats do the arrestin'."

He wagged his finger at Winthrop. "Now a bunch of guys have a great story about how they almost threw an officer in the ocean, and by the time they are old and gray, they'll swear they did throw a dumb ass officer into Buckner Bay."

The chuckles grew at Winthrop's expense, Larsen laughing the loudest, until the chaplain stood at his table and harrumphed.

Randolph leaned his head back, nodded at Winthrop and changed the subject. "My first class told me Sullivan and your guy, Mayer, almost got into it last night."

~

The ship's mail caught up with it, so the postal clerks held a mail call. Mary had written a warm letter about her activities and her affection

Flagship

for Winthrop. He spent a happy Tuesday, February 28, shopping for a four-track tape recorder, settling on a Sony at the exchange. He bought a couple of tapes to barter with. Johnny Mathis and Dusty Springfield ballads dominated.

Everyone bought four-tracks in WESTPAC that year. Crew members passed the tapes around, copied them, and thus taped pop music filled the *Eldorado's* spaces as a replacement for radio and TV shows not available at sea.

On March 1, the flagship was under way for Da Nang. On one of his watches Winthrop read the OOD message board. Phase II of operation Deckhouse VI concluded upon *Eldorado*'s arrival. The message reported the second phase killed 78 VC. The cost, another six Marines killed in action.

Just statistics, he thought, but for six families back in the States the body bags were real. It got old, the reports of the number of American dead, and the estimates of enemy dead. That thought took Winthrop to contemplate his own mortality. Life marches on. The dead Marines would have their names forever emblazoned on bricks in Parris Island, the place that turned them from young Americans into fighting men. Their bodies would arrive home with the Purple Heart and other medals. After a while, they would be forgotten.

President Johnson, the man whose strategy in Vietnam bounced back and forth between bombing the North and not bombing the North depending on the current force of the political winds, the man who forbade an invasion of the North, the man who commanded weapons that could end the war in an instant, instead sent thousands of soldiers to their deaths chasing a shadowy enemy through the jungle. He did it again and again. That president would enjoy a long life. And yet the future dead,

115

they still came to serve; Winthrop's fellow Americans, to serve in the meat grinder of Vietnam.

What kind of man was this who wouldn't allow his country to win and simply served up more Americans for slaughter?

With no answer for the president's actions, Winthrop found his own answer. *Do your duty.*

~

On the bridge at his battle station on the morning of March 6 Winthrop observed the scene as *Eldorado* entered Da Nang harbor buttoned up at general quarters, a precaution. A recent rocket attack on the port's Marine airbase by the North Vietnamese Army perked up the ship's security awareness. Both VC and NVA periodically attacked the base with soviet made rockets launched from the jungle outskirts of the city.

The calm blue sea, sandy beaches and waving palm trees belied the destruction at the base of a few days before. Something like 16 Marines and Airmen were killed in that attack.

Eldorado anchored. The boatswain passed the word. "Now secure from general quarters, secure the special sea and anchor detail, set condition Yoke," and the crew closed hatches. Material condition Yoke meant *enemy actives probable*. Most hatches were kept closed except when in use.

And Winthrop took over the watch, the recent rocket attacks on his mind. *Eldorado's* anchorage positioned her within range of the rockets used by the North. The flagship's mobility provided her best defense. It took some time for the VC to position the rockets for launch from the jungle north of the airfield, but the base remained a stationary target.

Eldorado moved. She lingered only a day or so each time she anchored at the base making a rocket attack difficult to stage.

The anchored ship drew other threats. Commander Webster, stationed aft at secondary conn during general quarters, came up to the bridge to brief Winthrop.

"Our intelligence reports possible attacks by swimmers," he said. "We're posting armed sentries and running an anti-swimmer picket boat, one of the LCVP's, just precautions. CIC will maintain radio contact with the picket."

He reviewed his notes, his face taut with concentration, and continued.

"Have your JOOD check on the sentries every few hours. Joe Trucker will coordinate with Nobel to get a couple of your first division boats in the water for the staff transportation. Hoffman in second division will get the *papa* boat launched. Expect some flight quarters on your watch too."

Noble arrived on the bridge next. "Got some watch changes for your approval. Got Spellman and Murray off to run our boats if needed. Staff guys will run the chief-of-staff gig."

Winthrop signed the document. "Mayer's pulling sentry duty, huh? You sure about that?"

"He's improved. He and Lee are buddies, don't like buddies on the same watch station."

"Good point."

All sailors received firearms training. Now, some of *Eldorado's* seamen would put the training to use protecting their ship. Third division gunner's mates provided them each with an M-1, old, but lethal.

Even with the sentries, *Eldorado* posted its regular port, starboard, and aft lookouts.

The Vietnamese enemy had never successfully attacked a US Navy ship. The agile destroyers, cruisers and carriers possessed formidable speed and weapons, but a tangible threat existed. The anchored flagship presented a juicy target with its WW II guns, lack of armor or speed, and outfitted only for a command and communications role.

Johnson maintained his professional approach on watch as he managed the rotation of the lookouts and other functions without prodding. Winthrop appreciated his competence. But the man retained a continuous cold demeanor toward Winthrop and other officers.

What would he do in a pinch?

The duty section stayed at high alert. Jay Dunston, his JOOD, made a periodic circuit of the ship to check on the sentries. His girlfriend back in the States failed to send him a timely letter from home, but as a good and loyal man he put aside his blues and plowed through his duties.

Winthrop called out the flight quarters detail on two occasions for helicopter landing and takeoff, both managed without incident by second division sailors. Crews running the first division booms lowered three boats, the chief-of-staff's gig, the captain's gig, and the officer's motor boat or OMB, for duty. The second division lowered one of its papa boats for use as the picket boat.

Just another watch in the combat zone, Winthrop reflected when at noon Randolph relieved him. He completed his log, signed it, climbed down the ladder to the main deck, and headed for the wardroom. The air conditioning worked well in the officer's lounge area, unlike his stateroom which stayed in a perpetual swelter, cooler than outdoors but not much.

118

He planned to plunk down in one of the black leather over-stuffed chairs and sip a cup of coffee with sugar and evaporated milk. Relax before lunch.

16

On the bridge, Winthrop supervised the watch the evening of March 12 as *Eldorado* steamed out of the combat zone toward Subic Bay for resupply. Two days in Subic meant a chance to see Mary. He recalled the conversation with Reilly as the print shop printed copies of the manual for replenishment underway. The availability of the UNREP manual to the ready group didn't preclude the return of the flagship to its home away from home this time.

This time.

Over the previous few weeks, Winthrop sensed an increase in the intensity of the flagship's activities. The resupply after a short period of operations loomed ominous for *Eldorado*'s future. And a stopover of only two days in Subic meant intensity in its own right.

The two-and-a-half-day transit to the Philippines seemed almost a pleasure cruise compared to the concentrated demands of ship handling the previous thirty days. It allowed Winthrop to ease up on his watch standing protocol. His new man Lee stood on the port lookout post and Johnson had walked aft for his periodic check on the stern lookout.

Winthrop gave the conn to Dunston and strolled over to chat with Lee. He lit a cigarette, offered one to the seaman, who declined. The breeze from the flagship's stately twelve knots in an otherwise calm sea pushed the smoke aft.

"Quiet evening for a change, huh?" Winthrop said.

"Yes sir," Lee responded with an upbeat tone in his voice. None of the lidded eye "I'm black and you're white" attitude he had the night of Owen's bad joke on the way over from the states.

Flagship

"Hear from your folks?"

Lee reached for his wallet, fumbled with it and pulled out a folded newspaper article from his hometown. A picture of Lee in his boot camp graduation uniform appeared under a headline "Local Man Serving on Flagship for Marine Amphibious Raid in Vietnam."

Good, Larsen's doing his job as PAO. Harley Larsen, for all his novice mistakes, was at least sending out press releases. The flagship's releases were sent by secret message to detachment Charlie, euphemistically nicknamed "dead Charlie" at the military assistance command, Vietnam, in Saigon. Navy intelligence officials there cleared the story of any classified material and the Navy journalists released it to the world. The fleet hometown news center, a key outlet for the detachment, placed the story in local newspapers around the US.

Servicemen far from home needed support like anyone else. That single story, sent to Lee by his parents, provided a lot.

Winthrop grinned, "Great article, bet your folks are proud."

"Yes, sir."

"Carry on," Winthrop said, flicked his cigarette overboard, and walked back to the wheelhouse feeling an uptick in his own moral. He thought of his parents. *They know we're out here.* Even in safe areas, the South China Sea had a cold loneliness about it. But the florescent glow of the old ship's wake seemed a bit warmer than usual.

~

Since the Navy did not provide any accommodation for a young man wishing to see his girlfriend, Winthrop was assigned deck department duty on the first day in port, a Tuesday, but he was able to call Mary and set a date for Wednesday. He took leave for that day.

121

Tuesday provided no rest. His day started with mustering the department, then breakfast. At officer's call, he received an assignment to organize a congo line of duty sailors for the supply department. Whether supplies came aboard by highline transfer at sea, by the ship's booms in port, or truckload on the pier, sailors were needed to carry individual packages down to the ship's storerooms. The best way to handle the hot dirty job was as old as the Navy. A line of men was formed beginning with the pile of supplies. The line passed individual packages hand to hand into the ship through its hatches, down its ladders, and along its passageways to the storeroom.

Lunch brought mail call and payday. The ship's disbursing officer had made an early morning trip and returned with an armed guard and cash for all hands. Winthrop's allotment to his home town bank to repay his student loan still left him with enough to spend on Mary the next day and perhaps keep some aside for foreign ports.

The afternoon found Winthrop discussing a broken part on one of the ship's davits with the second division's duty petty officer. *Eldorado*'s davits, one on the port quarter and one on the starboard quarter, each included two hoists which held a landing boat by the bow and stern. The boats, LCVPs, nicknamed "papa boats," could drive right up on a beach and flop open their flat bows. The crew could launch these boats faster than the forward booms could lower the more conventional boats used by officers. Thus, they were used in case of a man overboard and had to be kept workable. Breakdowns had to be fixed.

The engineering petty officer of the watch devised a simple workable solution for the davits. No matter what job came up aboard ship, the Navy had a trained sailor skilled at doing it. The engineering gang, second in size only to the deck gang could fix anything.

122

~

The following day, after breakfast Winthrop told the duty driver to drive him over to the base commander's house. "Official business," he explained to the driver. "Uh huh," the sailor responded.

Mary popped off the porch and greeted Winthrop with a kiss. The driver sped off.

"You got an Irish pennant," she said and pulled a loose thread off Winthrop's collar. Winthrop, developing another kind of Irish pennant, said, "Let's find a private place."

After, they showered and talked about the future.

"I'm thinking of going back to college this summer," Mary said.

"We might get back here once or twice in the meantime."

"Hope so."

He leaned back yet held her close around the waist, drank in her face and her scent, not her perfume, but her body fragrance, fresh, bread-like.

"*Eldorado* heads to the states in early July," Winthrop said, "I'll stop by your college on the way home to Syracuse."

"Will you forget me in all that time and skip coming to Ohio?"

"Ohio's right on my way. But I bet all those college boys will turn your head."

"Oh, I hope not."

The question of marriage started entering Winthrop's mind after his commissioning. The girlfriends he enjoyed in college were more casual affairs. Marriage never entered his head in those days. Of course college life was not a real world, more a matter of playing at life. What do I do about Mary, he thought?

And my whole future. He had no answer. He realized a need to think and plan for his life after the Navy. A few glimpses at his own mortality, like the near collision with the hospital ship, *Sanctuary,* focused his thoughts on these matters. Anything could happen.

Eldorado proceeded west to the combat zone the following day.

~

After a couple of days of consultations with various officials of the US and South Vietnamese military, the commander amphibious forces Pacific fleet ordered his flagship under way and made a series of anchorages south of Da Nang for further meetings: Chu Lai on March 8, Qui Nhon on the 9th, and Na Trang on the 10th. The vessel moved to material condition Yoke at each location.

Sentries, water-line lights and a picket boat completed the security at anchor. Although attack by small craft remained a threat, swimmers bothered Winthrop the most. Small craft were detectable by radar making them easy to spot. Swimmers rendered radar useless for security. The Viet Cong irregulars operated few boats, but a clandestine attack by underwater commandos fit their repertoire. If ever the flagship came under direct attack the most likely source other than jungle based rockets came from irregulars in the water. The situation demanded hypervigilance and the Navy provided it, but the demanding watch rotation pushed the crew's stamina to its maximum.

Sweltering hours of routine drudgery interspersed with four-hour stretches on duty stretched into days of anchoring, weighing anchor and steaming around off the Vietnam coast. Most of the men knew far less about each operation and *Eldorado*'s role than Winthrop. They did their jobs. They slept when they could.

Winthrop's daily grind filled with tedium. He skipped most evening movies, the only entertainment available and instead tried to keep up on his sleep. His smoking increased. He drank too much coffee. Mary's image drifted in and out of his head at times. Did their affair happen? Reality tended to fade with time. Her one letter was affectionate, but mail calls were few. *Eldorado*'s movements kept Mary's letters from catching up with him.

17

Operation Beacon Hill I commenced for Winthrop when General Quarters sounded at dawn on March 19. The day broke bright, the ocean calm as the Marines of the special landing force landed south of the Demilitarized Zone. From a half-mile at sea, Winthrop viewed the scene as the aroma of smokeless powder from a nearby destroyer reached his senses. Like a whiff of plasticine transported him back to kindergarten, odors similar to smokeless powder were destined to forever bring back the memory of Marine landings. Diluted over the water, the scent did not produce a gasping stench like the smell of burning tires, or the choke of wood smoke. More like fireworks on the fourth of July, the smell brought thoughts of patriotism and bravery.

The DMZ, as it was called, functioned much like a barrier for the US military and a welcome mat for the North. The armed forces couldn't go further north than the DMZ. Yet the North Vietnamese army moved south as if it didn't exist.

President Johnson's rules of engagement puzzled anyone with common sense. Winthrop's take: either his country was at war or not. The North Vietnamese followed no rules, yet the US military operated with restrictions. *Dumb.* The president sacrificed America's young men on the altar of the nutty war protestors. Servicemen died because of naïve, pot smoking, privileged kids.

He stood next to Dunston. "I'd like to get some of those brats protesting the war out in the jungle with those Marines."

"They'd shit their pants," Jay said. "Think they're cool. Real brave yelling and throwing stones at cops, who they know won't hurt them. Like to see how brave they'd be in a Marine platoon."

Winthrop stood on his toes to stretch the hard steel deck ache out of his legs. "After the last deployment I was in a cab, in uniform, heading for the airport. Had a free military standby flight back from home. Some puke in long hair, driving a pickup, pulled up alongside and screamed. Screamed, I tell ya, he didn't just shout, he screamed, 'You that anxious to kill?'"

"The jerk. Those pukes are the reason Johnson has all these rules of engagement. He's afraid he'll lose his job. Instead he is losing the war. He don't give a rats ass about the grunts or any of us."

Why Johnson dithered on bombing the North left Winthrop shaking his head. *It was the damn protestors.*

Johnson ordered bombing the jungle along the Ho Chi Minh trail. The bombing killed trees and created holes in the ground without stopping the North's aggression. Communist supplies and soldiers poured in along the trail like ants to an Italian picnic. The defoliants which the US sprayed destroyed plant life in great swaths, but didn't much help the war effort. Winthrop believed President Kennedy, had he lived, would not have done it this way.

The increase in US military intensity Winthrop had sensed during the flagship's return to Subic Bay now materialized as the Marine landing force found the enemy near Cua Viet, on March 21. They met and engaged a company sized component of the North Vietnamese Army.

Winthrop had gleaned this information as he read the detailed tactical results on the OOD secret message board. He learned the enemy withdrew after heavy fighting, leaving forty-three dead on the battlefield.

127

Once again the legendary US Marines demonstrated why they were held in so high regard. They fought through defensive trenches and tunnels and routed the enemy.

Days merged together as the flagship maintained station at sea in the area. One morning after breakfast Winthrop relieved Steve Taylor at 7:30 for the eight-to-twelve watch. The morning watch ran an extra half hour longer so the four-to-eight watch standers could eat breakfast before the wardroom and crew's mess closed at eight o'clock.

He had begun to notice that like the previous Deckhouse VI landing no fishing boats populated the waters. It was as if the locals had an inkling of the planned assault in advance. Of course, if they knew, the enemy knew.

He gave Jay Dunston the conn. The captain's orders required cruising on various courses and at various speeds in a ten mile by five mile rectangular area just off the coast. *Eldorado* provided ready access to the Admiral for the other ships of the ready group and the Marine commander of the landing forces. The radiomen in the com department kept busy. Even a tactical air control squadron came aboard to help vector F-4 Phantom aircraft air strikes and other air traffic in the area. The giant carrier USS *Kitty Hawk* provided the air resources. Other ships of the amphibious Navy cruised in the area.

No nation in the world could mount such displays of power 6,000 miles from its homeland. Winthrop took in the scene. Within view were the gray ships of the ARG, a dock landing ship, a tank landing ship, and the amphibious assault ship, *Iwo Jima,* capable of transporting and landing up to 1,000 Marines by chopper and boat. A destroyer ready to provide gunfire support cruised close to shore. The ships could reload the men now fighting on the beach, pull out, and land them somewhere else on short notice.

The bridge radio squawked: "*Eldorado, Eldorado,* over." Winthrop grabbed the handset. "This is *Eldorado,* over."

"I Corps chopper two inbound."

"*Eldorado*, roger," Winthrop said.

He turned to Johnson. He said, "Pipe flight quarters."

Then to Dunston, "Jay, get us a relative wind across the bow."

Dunston went into action. He had a relative wind of fourteen knots blowing from about five degrees off the port bow. Eldorado was moving at 10 knots. Slowing would move the relative wind further to the port but slow it. A turn to starboard would change the direction without slowing it so much. He needed a course change not a speed change.

He ordered the helm, "right standard rudder." And the old girl responded as Dunston watched the relative wind indicator. When the wind direction moved to about 45 degrees off the port bow, he spoke, "Steady up on course zero-nine-five."

Winthrop reviewed in his mind the actions to take in case of a disaster. Best to think these things through, he figured, so if the chopper crashed, his response could be immediate. He would stop the ship and call out the man-overboard team. If the crash caused a fire on the ship, or the chopper started burning on the water nearby, he would call out the damage control team, the fire team, and the hospital corpsmen. On Navy vessels men were organized into special teams and drilled for emergencies. If Winthrop called out such a group it would respond in an instant. Such was the state of *Eldorado's* readiness.

He could count on the men.

He lit a cigarette.

129

After the chopper took off again, the old man strolled out on the bridge. Dunston was in the process of ordering a course change back to 020 degrees as the ship was in the southern part of its steaming area.

The captain motioned Winthrop over to where he stood on the port wing of the bridge.

"How's Mister Dunston doing?" he said.

"Fine, he's a good man, the best I could have as JOOD."

"We need another OOD. Steve Taylor will take over as acting ops department head. Edger's going state-side. I'm thinking of qualifying Mister Dunston for the bridge watch."

Winthrop caught a bit of distain in the captain's voice when he mentioned the ops boss. He hadn't called him "commander," a term used for a respected lieutenant commander, normally addressed as "mister." Nor had he even called him "mister." Instead his used his last name.

"I'll sleep soundly if Jay has the mid-watch." Winthrop said.

"Thought so. Thank you, Fred." The captain turned and walked back toward his sea cabin.

Word gets around aboard ship. The men observe how an OOD or JOOD conducts himself. It is not long before the crew labels an OOD a strict watch stander, a loose watch stander or even incompetent. The word filters up to the old man, *always*.

The word on Jay Dunston said he was competent.

~

At noon Winthrop relinquished the watch and went below for lunch. The regular guys at his table were eating. He joined them, picked up his napkin ring and removed the linen napkin, sat back. Ocampo, the table steward, brought a fresh glass of water and a cup of coffee, went off and returned with rice and a meat and vegetable stew. Winthrop took large helpings.

The conversation turned to Mister Edger.

"He got passed over for commander. That's why he's leaving," Merlin Chandler said. "The chief engineer told me about it."

"He's outta Annapolis, ain't he?" Chips Beasley said.

"Yeah, this time he thought he might make it, but it was the third time, so he's gotta go. He's got his twenty-years, so at least he can retire. He could stay for the rest of this cruise, but I guess he figures he'll be better off leaving now."

"He's thick as a brick," Winthrop couldn't help saying. "The ship will be better off."

"He played football at the academy," Chandler said. "Maybe that's the reason . . . for his slow mind machinery."

Winthrop stayed quiet, thinking Edger might be the reason CIC operated so poorly. Taylor, as Edger's CIC officer, stayed tied up on the bridge, Edger's call. The radar men in CIC had lost their edge, because of Edger, Winthrop figured.

~

The flagship returned the admiral to Da Nang on March 23. The crew set material condition Yoke with nighttime waterline lights, and a defensive picket boat. No liberty.

Lt. Cmdr. Edger dressed all in black, approached Winthrop on the port wing of the bridge where he stood leaning against the compass ring pedestal. Topped with a telescope, the directional input came from a central ship's gyroscope. Quartermasters sighted bearings of coastal landmarks with the device to plot the ship's location in coastal waters. It provided an uncomfortable support for a sleepy Winthrop.

131

Bored, patting the .45 caliber Ithaca pistol strapped to his side, Dunston having moved out on the weather decks to check on the sentries, Winthrop reacted with surprise at the sight of the black clad man.

"Hey, Fred, come here," The man whispered. It was Lt. Cmdr. Edger.

He wore black shoes, black pants, black turtleneck sweater, black knit watch cap, and black grease under his eyes.

"Mr. Edger?" Winthrop asked.

"Evening, Fred," Edger said. "I'm going to test the sentries, sneak up on 'em."

"Captain know you're doing this?" Winthrop shocked himself saying that. This was the senior watch officer, but the concept seemed so bizarre. *Why sneak up on armed sentries?*

Winthrop stood OOD watches because the old man trusted his judgement in any situation. But this, the senior watch officer, Winthrop's senior in rank but not in position, put him in a delicate situation. *Was Edger completely fucking crazy?*

Winthrop could order him to stop, but Edger had informed him. He had come up to the darkened bridge and told him his plans. It created a delicate protocol challenge. Winthrop as OOD commanded everyone on the ship exclusive of the captain, but if he interfered with a senior officer and the third in command, he had better be right.

"Jay Dunston is checking on them right now," he said, "so you don't have to." Winthrop played for time as his thoughts reeled through his options: Call the captain out on the bridge; Tell Edger "Hell no, not on my watch;" Look the other way and hope no one gets shot.

He head still spinning through possibilities, Winthrop heard Edger say, "Huh, oh yeah."

Flagship

Lieutenant Commander Edger, Annapolis graduate, a man who had served his country for twenty years, including the Inchon amphibious landing, slapped his forehead with his open palm and said, "Guess I better not. Forget it."

He walked inside the pilot house, through the quartermaster shack, as Winthrop, cautious, followed him. He took the inside passage between the captain's cabin and the XO's quarters and headed down below toward officer's quarters. Winthrop decided not to follow.

Like Johnson had done during the Pacific crossing, using Deep South black lingo on the 1 MC because of Owen's bad joke, Edger had screwed up. But once again only Winthrop understood all the details. He decided never to speak of the incident. *Best for the Navy. The guy has earned a pass with his long service.*

18

Eldorado headed off to Taiwan for rest and recreation, R&R as the Navy called it, and to show the flag. The crew observed Easter Sunday at sea on March 26 and made Keelung, Taiwan the next day. The vessel tied up to a buoy in the harbor. The commander-in-chief of the Nationalist Chinese navy paid a courtesy call on the commander amphibious forces pacific fleet. All the off duty crew members secured liberty passes and headed for Taipei, some to the restaurants, many to the brothels in the Peitou district.

Winthrop, Dunston, Randolph, and Ensign Larsen chipped in for a cab. The driver kept taking them to whorehouses until they asked him to drive them by the US Embassy. There they found a young American woman walking out the front of the embassy. Blonde, blue eyed, pretty, she told the cabbie in Chinese what they wanted, a restaurant, not a brothel. He took them to the Taipei Theater Restaurant.

The lavish restaurant featured a large menu of exotic delights. The stage was empty for the lunch hour but waiters and waitresses scurried around the crowed hall. The hostess showed the young officers a table on the second level balcony. Winthrop chose a thousand-year old egg and offset the item with something he assumed palatable, the chicken soup. The egg smelled of sulfur but tasted delicious. The soup included the chicken's feet. Winthrop took few sips of soup and wolfed down the egg, finishing his entrée. Dessert tasted better.

The crew enjoyed the visit and created no trouble on the beach. Winthrop and Randolph kept their three adversaries, Sullivan, Mayer, and

Lee on different watch schedules so that Sullivan didn't go on liberty the same days as Lee or Mayer.

~

Nobel

The Chinese girl, about twenty, Nobel guessed, with smooth, ivory skin and the thin, long-limbed kind of body he favored, caught his eye. She stood with a group of hostesses wearing shorts and bikini tops in a plush selection area which included several levels. The hotel sparkled, none of the shabby and grimy appointments of typical whore houses in the Far East. US servicemen pulling R&R in Taiwan enjoyed the world-class delights of the Peitou district, a fabulous perk assuming one could survive Vietnam long enough to get R&R.

He selected the woman and together they took an elevator to his room. In a well-orchestrated maneuver she undressed him and led him into the bathroom where she removed her clothes and drew water in an oversized tub.

Aroused, he didn't object to her ministrations which amounted to an examination of his equipment. Satisfied he wasn't diseased, she slipped into the tub and he joined her.

The bathroom shined with cleanliness. Nobel took it all in. From the heated towel racks flush with fluffy towels to the ample floor plan, the glossy white tiles, and wall-length mirrors, the cleanliness impressed him.

This is a classy place.

The Peitou district attracted businessmen from around the world. Nobel reveled in his fortune. *The Navy has its advantages.*

He wanted to freeze his life and finish the rest of it in this idyllic place. Close enough to heaven for government work, he figured. But his own experience with women had taught him that a few moments of extreme delight like he now experienced came with days and nights of conflict, lies, deceit and frustration, not a good trade. His previous wife and almost wife both deceived him and left him feeling used, abused and cynical.

The Navy redeemed him, but he faced his career end if he couldn't get the CPO rank. He wondered what life would be like if he retired back in his home town of Caribou. He dreamed of buying a small place in the woods to live out his life in solitude—a long time to live with a small retirement and not much to do. He estimated he could live another thirty years. But fishing the brooks and hunting the woods of northern Maine could hold his interest only so long.

He shook his head. *Concentrate on the now.* He lay naked, sprawled out on his back on the king-sized bed, and the girl was down to his belly with little kisses . . .

~

Johnson

Taiwan, he had visited the place before on a couple of R&Rs when he served with the PBRs. He remembered his wife's admonishment. *Stay out of the whore houses, Jerome.* The pull of desire challenged his resolve. His regular liberty buddies, some second-and third-class black petty officers flashing rolls of cash, slicked down and wearing cologne headed for the Peitou hotels.

He recalled the Chinese girls' ivory skin, not like the black girls back home. The Chinese women who worked in the fields in rural areas developed sun-darkened skin, but those privileged to work indoors, including prostitutes, retained their natural lighter skin tones. He shook his head to get rid of the pictures in his mind.

136

Johnson took the liberty boat to the fleet landing and a cab to the China Seas EM Club run by the military assistance advisory group Taiwan. The trip got him off the ship for a while without the temptations of the Taipei night life.

He sat alone with a beer and a hamburger. Bode, the third class in his division came in with a couple of seamen from his regular detail in first division. Mayer, another white sailor, and two other black sailors whom Johnson recognized, were with the group. They spotted him and waved him over.

Bode, grinning said, "Not out whorin' with your buddies?"

"Nope, rather not get my balls cut off by the wife when I get home."

Mayer spoke up, a feeling of camaraderie surging through him, "Lee says ya from Deeetroit City," he said. "Motown, *Stop in the Name of Love*. Ya ever meet the Supremes?"

"No, no went right in the Navy from high school. Leticia made me. Used to cruise with a guy we called Downtown Charlie Brown. Know him?

Mayer sat back. "Huh, no," he said.

"Where you from, Mayer?"

"North Carolina."

"Not much of an accent."

"No, Mom raised me. She's from the North."

Mayer changed the subject, his voice unsteady. "My daddy helped build this here ship. Last one he worked on before he went off to war."

His face flushed, he added, "He was missing in action." Eyes misting, he added, "Normandy."

He hadn't wanted to bring up his old man. The thought always brought tears, but he never wanted to talk about his mom either. She relied on him in her crazy way. He stuttered, tried to change the subject again.

"*Eldorado . . .*" he said. "Ya know, ya know she carried the flag for the landing at Iwo Jima."

Johnson caught it. *He almost bawled.*

"Yeah, she been around," he said. She was at Inchon too."

He took a swig from his beer.

"My old man works for the city. Always has, always will. I wanted something better, so I joined the Navy. It been good for me."

He stretched, avoiding Mayer's eyes, turned and looked toward Bode.

"How about you, Bode?"

"I'm from a place called Lost Creek. It's in Wyomin'. Joined the Navy to see the world." He raised his beer. "Here's one for the US Navy."

After two more rounds Bode and his group decided to go into town.

Johnson headed back to the ship thinking, *Mayer's parents . . . a soft spot.* Johnson now figured Lee being black needn't be the reason for a fight between Sullivan and Mayer. When Sullivan heard Mayer's folks formed the essence of his psyche he would badger Mayer about them unmercifully. And Mayer would fight.

~

Mayer

His mother never recovered from the loss of his dad in the over 20 years since his birth and since the Army reported his dad missing in action on Omaha Beach. *She's a basket case.*

138

Flagship

He grew up enduring her obsessions and weird requirements. She cleaned and recleaned the bedding after, at age five, he sat on his dad's side to wake her up. She kept Dad's half made up, ready for him to come home, the covers turned down, and everything, while she slept on her side of the bed careful not to disturb his side.

He believed at first, thinking any day he might see his dad walk through the front door. By age ten he realized his mom was bat-shit crazy and his old man would never come home. Mayer began to doubt his father ever existed. Some of his school chums told him women who screwed soldiers and sailors during the war without marrying them often told their illegitimate kids the old man died in battle or was missing in action.

He confronted her about being a bastard, but she showed him her marriage certificate and his birth certificate. Too poor to have a full blown wedding, she could show him no pictures of the ceremony. But she did find some old snapshots of the two of them together.

Mayer worked part time during high school to help out. Showing up late or calling in sick cost his mom many menial jobs over those years. She started drinking early on. His mom degenerated into a crazy old hag with unkempt hair. She rarely washed. *But he loved her.* By his sophomore year, she moved the two of them to a single room in a boarding house. One night the following year, after he turned seventeen, he got her to sign off on his enlistment papers when she was plastered.

He had sent most of his pay home, made few friends and tended to recluse himself and sneak around, hard to do on *Eldorado.* Now, he met with the chaplain once a week. He found a buddy in Lee, his first friend in the Navy, and tonight he had joined the guys on liberty. *Shouldn't have mentioned my dad . . . or my mom. Can't handle that yet. Maybe someday.*

~

On the morning of April 1 the ship called out the sea and anchor detail. Winthrop hurried to the bridge. There he learned that an officer in the supply department failed to return to the ship.

Sunlight glinted off the bay waters, reflecting the blue of the clear sky of Keelung. Why ruin such a day by not returning to the ship Winthrop wondered. The Navy took some risk of an accident befalling a sailor at each liberty port, yet the need to blow off steam made liberty ports ideal for upping the crew's moral and improving performance at sea. In *Eldorado*'s case up to 450 men flooded ashore at each port and they were not headed for church.

A guy could be court-martialed for missing a movement. Enlisted men in foreign seaports got themselves in trouble sometimes, but an officer? Perhaps it was foul play. No one knew. The captain fumed.

As *Eldorado* loaded its boats, readying to cast off from the buoy, the admiral's barge returned. It pulled alongside with a sheepish young ensign aboard. If a man could pick the most conspicuous way to return late from liberty, certainly few could exceed arriving aboard the admiral's personal craft. The captain made him stand right there in the boat, with its crew, in full view of the whole ship, as the boom operator hoisted it to the rack on deck.

Eldorado steamed out of Keelung leaving the iconic statute of Chang Kai-shek, fist raised to mainland China, in its wake and carrying her own celebrity of sorts. But the supply department ensign was no celebrity with the captain.

Flagship

Later, to some restrained chuckles in the wardroom, the red faced, errant officer slid into his chair at another table and bent over his lunch. Winthrop learned the guy received a written reprimand from the old man and restriction to the ship at the next port of call. His two days at a hotel with a Chinese hostess who bathed and screwed him, expertly and often, in his words was "worth it."

19

In a message received on the same day *Eldorado* sailed from Taiwan, the brass judged operation Beacon Hill a success. The Communists lost 334 fighters, or so the official body count reported. The cost, Winthrop mused, ran too high; 230 Marines wounded and 29 killed in action. *The brass called it a success. How could the loss of 29 Marines be called a success?*

Winthrop didn't believe the enemy body count. Anyway the enemy could field legions more. The US control of the area the SLF cleared out would only last as long as the grunts stayed in the field. What was the point? The Westmoreland concept of escalation until the North called uncle, endorsed by the president, treated the Marines, indeed all the in-country grunts, as cannon fodder. The United States possessed the ability to win so much easier and without so much loss of good men. *Bring the war to the North. Bomb the shit out of them.* Winthrop knew escalation could win over the long term, but the strategy treated the troops callously. *They were our countrymen for Christ's sake.*

The amphibious ready group, special landing force tandem proved itself so adept, the military decided to double the concept. The flagship sailed south to Okinawa. Off the coast of the Japanese island, the flag staff and some ship's company crew members refined the new strategy. They created special landing force Bravo, a twin for the existing Alpha landing force.

To test the concept's feasibility *Eldorado* and the admiral's staff directed a dummy double landing to check communications and other details. No liberty for the crew.

Flagship

After the reorganization and dummy run-through, replacements arrived and the battered Alpha Marines received a welcome stand down. The flagship sailed for Hong Kong on April 8 to show the flag and offer her crew some R&R.

Typhoon Violet developed in the ship's path, as if providence objected to *Eldorado*'s departure from the war.

The captain and navigator played a deft game plotting a course to skirt the monster typhoon. The flagship instituted the heavy weather bill. The captain ordered outside decks closed except for emergencies and watch standers. Deck division sailors rigged lines fore and aft along the centerline as emergency handholds for anyone who had to venture outside. The stern lookout moved from the fantail to the flight deck. The old girl buttoned up against the weather.

Men walking below decks extended both hands out from their sides. The passageways demonstrated the value of their narrow design. They provided support as the ship heaved and rolled, groaning with the stresses of storm waves.

Winthrop handled the heavy weather well. He found the steep rolling and pitching of the vessel invigorating, and he suffered no seasickness. Not all the crew responded the same as he. The heads filled with retching sailors.

On the eight-to-twelve watch Winthrop witnessed green water thundering over the bow as a giant swell hit. When the bow bobbled up the steel hull groaned and encountered a smaller wave splashing foam over the bow and on down to the forward well deck. White water washed over the bow and rolled onto the weather decks with regularity, but the green wall of water gave Winthrop a start. Eldorado's hull, very similar to the mass produced Liberty ships of World War II, relied on welded steel plates in its construction. *How sound is this old hull?*

The wind indicator showed a solid sixty knots with slightly higher gusts. The wave tops flattened in the blow. The cold, hard, salt smell of the storm at sea ached in Winthrop's sinus and funneled primitive urges to seek refuge where none existed. The high seas, now he understood the term.

Reacting to the light rain, unlike the torrents some earlier watches experienced, Winthrop repositioned the forward lookouts to their regular stations perched out on the wings of the bridge. The captain had called them into the wheelhouse on the earlier watch.

Eldorado's course engaged the swells on her starboard bow, the best track in a storm, though not the most direct course to Hong Kong.

Lee, huddled in the port lookout station, saw it first. He pointed and shouted on the sound-powered phone: "There's a loose wire stay on the gig."

The bridge talker called out to Winthrop, "Port lookout reports a loose wire holding the gig."

Winthrop stepped out from the hatch. He leaned forward and held the cold edge of the grey steel barrier extending along the edge and breadth of the bridge deck. He examined the captain's gig. The boat moved with each swell, not a lot, but enough to alarm. If that boat or any other one tore loose in this weather, it could damage the other boats, the booms, and the superstructure before tumbling over the side. A first division responsibility, the gig, his own men had loaded it after the Okinawa visit. *Crap.*

He stepped inside and dialed the captain on the bridge phone. Ridgway answered, "Capt'n."

144

"Sir we got a loose stay wire on your gig. I think we need to send a couple seamen out there to tighten it up."

"I'll step out to the bridge."

He came through the quartermaster shack into the wheel house, took Winthrop's binoculars, bent over the rail, and examined the flapping guy wire.

"Looks like a turnbuckle loosened from all this rock 'n roll 'n," the old man said. "Go ahead and handle it. I'll be in my cabin if you need me."

"Aye, sir," Winthrop said and turned to Johnson. "Call Nobel up here."

Johnson blew his pipe, "Boatswain Mate First Class Nobel to the bridge."

~

Nobel got a couple of sailors out on the forward boat deck with life jackets and life lines attached to the centerline rigging with snap clamps. They tightened the guy wire.

The situation had called for notifying the captain. The officer of the deck possessed complete authority to do such things on his own. He qualified for his position because of his knowledge and good judgement. If the OOD reacted to an unusual threat without consulting the old man, when sufficient time existed to obtain his advice or a decision, the OOD might find himself off the watch list or worse. Although he held near absolute power over the crew while on watch, he could not exercise command without judiciousness which demanded consultation with the captain when possible in unusual circumstances. The fine edge between the necessity to act and the necessity to call the old man occurred rarely during peace time cruising. In the combat zone situations arose more often.

145

The rule for the OOD stated: if in doubt, call the captain, but if necessary, act, and then call the captain. Winthrop lived with the rule. It hovered in his consciousness during the near collision with *Sanctuary*. He chose to act. The crisis resolved, he then decided not to wake the captain. This test of his acumen hung over all his actions on the bridge.

~

After his watch Winthrop sat at his regular table in the wardroom for lunch. He grabbed a piece of fresh white bread, placed it under his plate and squished it down. A crash on the floor next to the head table brought the wardroom's attention to the chaplain's dish lying smashed on the deck. A steward scurried over to clean up the mess. The chaplain let out an uncharacteristic, "Crap." A loose chair on the other side of the room slid sideways to the far bulkhead as the ship rolled and yawed.

Better the stewards serve sandwiches for lunch, Winthrop figured. But the men passed around a bowl of rice, and Ocampo managed to keep his balance and serve the *giniling*. It seemed whenever you asked a steward, "What's for lunch?" he would answer "giniling," and chuckle. The Filipino stewards were upbeat, happy guys, but the crew's mess deck offered hamburgers, steaks, and French fries. Not the wardroom mess. Giniling a loose Tagalog term, meant hash or stew. Once Winthrop asked the chief steward a black guy, why they couldn't get something different for lunch. The chief offered frog legs and chitlins, and laughed.

The officers chipped in once a month to pay for the food in the wardroom mess. They controlled the menu through the wardroom president, usually a lieutenant or above appointed by the XO. But in practice the mess president, because of pressing duties, often abdicated the menu selection to the chief steward, who let the Filipinos, expert at cooking with rice, plan the menu.

146

The table conversation turned to *Eldorado*'s seaworthiness. Ensign Larsen mentioned the radarmen in CIC devised a "roll-o-meter," to measure the roll. They hung a piece of string with a weight on the end off a status board and they drew degree indications with a grease pencil. Larsen said the device hit thirty degrees a few times.

"These ship types have a strong righting angle," Merlin Chandler said. "They can handle a storm."

Winthrop's vague understanding of the physics of righting rolling ships came from one of his classes at officer candidate school. Since he majored in business in college the engineering stuff brought his grade average at OCS down to 2.8. He managed the engineering curriculum through rote memorization and a friendly chief petty officer who taught the class just before the final exam and gave everyone the gouge. He went through each question and gave the answer. A bunch of busy ballpoints scratched down the information, and the officer candidates memorized all the answers that night.

Winthrop remembered learning from a seamanship class that some liberty ships cracked in half in North Atlantic storms during World War II because of bad welds.

"How about the liberty ships?" he said. "*Eldorado* uses the same hull design."

"They always check the hull when we're in dry dock," Chandler said. We checked it on the last rotation in the States. Our ship is solid. You can count on it."

20

Because of the storm delay Hong Kong hosted *Eldorado* for only a short stay. Arriving and anchoring on April 12 she departed April 16 allowing only two full days of liberty. The place, a modern international city, did not cater to visiting warships in the way other Far East ports did. Expensive eating and drinking places quickly extracted the limited cash from visiting sailors. Prostitutes were non-existent or far above the crew's price range.

After an uncomfortable storm wracked trip to the port and with the prospect of leaving for the combat zone in a couple of days, the crew enjoyed little in the way of R&R. Several bought one of the famed Hong Kong custom tailored suits or pairs of custom shoes. Time was short, and some men were swindled by shopkeepers promising to mail the completed custom item and never doing so.

Winthrop bought custom black civilian dress shoes from a fellow known as "no squeak Young," and picked them up just before departure. They squeaked.

~

By April 22 his ship lingered off the South Vietnam coast near the border between Quang Tri province and Thua Thien province for operation Beacon Star. Special Landing Force Bravo got the call for this landing. The assault order, a secret message issued only twelve hours or so before the landing, sidestepped the enemy's regular intelligence sources. The brass was getting serious.

Eldorado steamed in and out of Da Nang, anchoring there on April 19, 23, 25, and April 29 as she bounced from the Beacon Star amphibious objective area to her Da Nang anchorage and back again. Choppers came and went, the flight quarters crew getting a workout. One in three watches prevailed, along with waterline lights at night and an anti-swimmer picket boat.

The greatest enemy threat to the anchored flagship came from the water. The picket boat might detect surface swimmers. It used a search light and circled the ship at regular intervals, but Winthrop questioned the boat's ability to catch enemies approaching underwater. Although the waterline lights might detect them before they could board, Winthrop feared NVA commandos with bubble-free rebreathing devices and limpet mines. They could approach without detection. *Eldorado* changed anchorages often. Against underwater swimmers, Winthrop figured, perhaps that was her best defense.

With the operations officer gone, Winthrop noticed an improvement in CIC support, but by then he had developed a strong sense for the ships in the area and how to maneuver among them without CIC feeding him course and speed information. He and the other watch officers kept a grease pencil track of the ships by marking their blips on the radar screen and passing the information on watch to watch. CIC did help by identifying some of the contacts.

Intelligence messages posted on the bridge starting warning of possible attack by small craft so the flag introduced a challenge procedure. The bridge watch aboard each vessel in the task force received a secret, hand-held manual computer consisting of a small wheel which spun inside a palm-sized holder. One would spin the wheel to the date of the month and read out a two letter code in a small window. Vessels challenged responded with the two letters. The flag issued a new device each month or as needed. The gadget reminded Winthrop of a plastic secret coding device he once got in a box of cereal.

When underway, ship handling intensity increased at night and Winthrop began to feel the cold grip of fear deep inside as he readied for a late night watch. The fear peaked at times of fatigue. On those occasions, he doubted he was up to the job.

He pushed himself through the doubt by picturing the Marines on the beach. *What were those poor devils facing?* The trepidation crested as he arrived on the darkened bridge, viewed the situation, sensed the shadowy movements of the watch standers, and heard the creaks and groans of the maneuvering flagship, and the radio conversations from other units of the ARG.

Once briefed by the off-going watch officer and assuming the watch, the bridge activity engulfed Winthrop. He spotted contacts, ordered them challenged by the signal bridge, established their identity, maneuvered to avoid other friendly vessels and to maintain station in the ship's assigned night steaming zone. The fear left. Coffee, cigarettes and adrenaline took over.

The day watches ran less intense. The fatigue eased in the sunlight. Just the feel of the sun on his face gave him a boost. Clear contacts were visible, no longer the vague hunks of blackness as they existed in the darken ship environment. He conducted flight quarters for arriving and departing choppers with confidence. The day watches rejuvenated him.

~

Toward the end of April the wardroom guys at Winthrop's table spotted some mysterious tiny black spots in the rolls served with lunch.

His taste unaffected, Winthrop wolfed down a couple, hot with the fresh butter melting and dripping.

Chips held a roll up to his glasses, examined the tidbits, and advised the table, "Weevils, Them little buggers' eggs tend to hatch in the tropics."

Larsen stopped in mid bite. "Bugs? We're eating bugs?"

The old hands, Chips Beasley and Merlin Chandler, nodded together.

"Usually happens during a WESTPAC cruise," Chandler said. "They don't hurt you, protein, you know."

Randolph put down his half eaten roll. "I'll pass."

Nothing more was said.

A few weeks later the captain heard about it.

The word came over the 1 MC. "Supply department head to the captain's cabin, on the double."

A sailor had written home and his parents contacted their local congressman who called the chief of naval operations. By the time the complaint reached the captain through the chain of command weevils in the flour became a cause célèbre.

A chastised supply department head pulled all the ship's flour sacks for examination. He ordered his sailors to toss most over the side. Dinner rolls and baked bread became hard to find on *Eldorado*. The crew awaited the next resupply. Funny, Winthrop observed, how you take simple things for granted until none are available.

The incident produced an unusual perk for Winthrop. The captain decreed that henceforth all OODs finishing a watch would eat their next meal on the mess decks. Winthrop found the mess deck food, laden with stuff like steaks, French fries, hamburgers, and navy beans, a welcome respite from the rice dishes the stewards concocted for the officers in the wardroom.

~

Eldorado returned to Subic Bay May 2 and stayed until May 15, during which time fresh flour and other staples came aboard, and the ship refueled.

Lieutenant Commander Edger left the ship for the States.

While the flagship resupplied, the brass ordered Marines of special landing force Bravo, fighting near the beach, flown inland to help beleaguered troops in what became known as the first battle of Khe Sanh. The cost ran high, 71 died in battle and 349 suffered wounds. Five Navy hospital corpsmen serving as medics died in the engagement.

The results disturbed Winthrop. The losses illustrated the difficulty of a free country in conducting war. The more the president and his top advisors dithered, the more dissidents opposed the war. Young people terrified of being drafted and others with varying motives organized and threw political monkey wrenches into the effort. Thus, the country entered a deadly stalemate. Like a truck stuck in a mud hole, its driver with his foot on the accelerator, and the tires spewing muck, the US created an image of imposing power, getting nowhere. The Vietnam War was America's mud hole, her dead and maimed countrymen the spew.

Indeed, an enormous mud hole described President Johnson's grand failure. His decision to declare all-out war via the Gulf of Tonkin resolution may have been wise, or maybe not, depending on one's politics. But once he tied the military's hands and refused to permit the use of tactics that would allow quick and overwhelming victory, he doomed many innocent patriots to useless injury and death. And, Winthrop believed in his core, those young men where the county's best.

152

Flagship

The US would long suffer from Johnson's blundering. He destroyed the best segment of US citizens, permitting the flawed and misinformed, arrogant in their self-righteousness, to carry on the country's business, and leaving the surviving warriors, the abused and maligned future veterans, bitter, frustrated and wounded in their souls.

Lying on the shore with Mary near the White Rock Beach Hotel, Winthrop gave voice to these thoughts. His eyes closed, his back in the warm sand, he had let loose in a stream-of-consciousness to a quiet Mary.

"It's just a damn mess," Winthrop said.

Mary squeezed his hand. "You aren't going to protest the war are you?"

"No, that's not the point at all."

He rolled on the sand. Propped up on his elbow, he gazed at her. The beauty in her face always startled him.

"You're the only good thing to come out of this."

She kissed him.

21

By May 15, *Eldorado* steamed back toward the war zone.

Nearing the coast on May 17, *Eldorado,* without specific orders plowed west; with Winthrop on the bridge for the 2000 to 2400 watch. A second-class Winthrop hadn't seen before stepped on the bridge and handed him a message.

"Something for the OOD message folder, sir."

It was labeled "Secret."

"Haven't seen you before."

"Yes, sir. I was in com translating a Morse code SOS, so I figured I'd bring this up instead of the messenger. Get some fresh air."

"SOS?"

"Some ship way south of us. We referred it to the Indonesian Navy."

"Didn't know com did that."

"All the time sir."

"What's your name sailor?"

"Wyatt, sir, Radioman Second Class, Robert Wyatt."

"Thank you Wyatt."

Winthrop looked at the document as he walked over to a simple clip board with binder rings which hung over the chart table. The message was brief, clear.

SECRET—Operation Beau Charger and Belt Tight. Flagship and Amphibious Ready Group ordered to anchor 0600 18 May at AOA . . .

Flagship

The amphibious objective area for the attack, the Ben Hai River, was located in the demilitarized zone, previously off limits.

At the designated time special landing forces Alpha and Bravo landed by sea, storming ashore for operations Beau Charger and Belt Tight.

After general quarters the following day Winthrop stayed on the bridge for the eight-to-twelve watch, relieving GQ OOD Joe Trucker, who delivered the regular update of operations.

"It's not in the written orders," Trucker said, "but the old man told me to stay away from that little point of land up ahead. He wants us to stay at least ten thousand yards from it."

"What's with that?" Winthrop said.

"NVA artillery over there fired on one of our destroyers early this morning. The captain thinks our guys return fire destroyed the gun emplacement, but he's not sure. Said, 'stay away.'"

"Okay, got it," Winthrop said, saluted and added, "I relieve you, sir."

Under a cloudless sky and a climbing temperature, *Eldorado* plowed through calm waters at a stately ten knots. A couple of the ARG ships cruised in the distance.

Winthrop's new JOOD Harley Larsen arrived on the bridge.

~

Nobel

Nobel grabbed Bode after chow and said, "Come on, help me check the boat stays."

Bode, puzzled, said, "Yeah, okay."

Out on deck Nobel gripped the aft stay on the admiral's barge shook it, moved forward. "Check the other side, Bode," he said.

155

He stood in front of the barge, out of hearing range from the bridge where Lee stood port lookout. He motioned the third-class over to join him.

"How's Mayer doin'?"

"He's okay."

"Hoffman over in second division tells me Sullivan has been making noises about Mayer being a nigger lover."

"Yeah, Sullivan and Mayer had that run-in at a club in Okinawa. Remember, Sullivan tried to start a fight with Lee, but Mayer stood up for him. You an' Hoffman busted it up before they threw any punches."

"That's all?"

Bode cocked his head.

"He and Lee are buddies."

"So what's Sullivan's problem?"

"He's a bully, an ass. If it weren't Mayer, he'd pick on someone else. He thinks Mayer is Jewish."

"Is he?"

"Na, I think he's German."

"So Sullivan hates anyone who ain't Irish? Can Mayer fight?"

"I don't know. He's tough but screwed up. Confront him, he's the kind of guy would either whimper or kill you depending on his mood. He's seeing the chaplain on the sly. Lee likes him, says Mayer knows about bein' poor."

"Yeah," Nobel said, "Mayer needed a buddy. He's a better sailor now."

Nobel leaned against the boom, pushed his white hat to the back of his head.

"Sullivan wants to strike for the print shop. Lee's got Winthrop and Johnson supporting him for the same slot."

"So why don't he rag on Lee?" Bode said.

"He's afraid of Slim."

"Oh yeah," Bode said. "Johnson and that razor he carries. He scares me too."

"Sullivan thought he had it made," Nobel said, "Reilly and him being from South Boston. But when Lee got involved, Reilly kicked the decision up the chain of command. Edger was expected to decide, but now he's off the ship."

"So what am I supposed to do?"

"Be their buddy, hang out with them."

"I hang with all the guys, anyway."

"Do a little more. Better two white guys are buddies with Lee than one."

This is getting complicated. Nobel sighed.

"Sullivan thinks he can shake things up. Start rumors about them and slide into the print shop. Figures no one will take a chance on Lee if they think he likes boys, ya know what I mean?"

"Christ, I don't know . . ."

"There's more. For some reason Sullivan's picked on him since Mayer berthed with second division. Thinks Mayer stole some of his money. Started calling him Weasel."

~

Nobel wasn't adverse to breaking regulations. He and Hoffman of second division risked court martial when they organized the shower scrub that cleaned up Mayer's personal hygiene. Someone else swiped Mayer's uniforms to teach him a lesson.

157

Winthrop took no action on the shower incident and made no effort to find the culprits who stole Mayer's uniforms. Nobel gave the officer credit for common sense. An investigation of either event would have taken hours of the officer's time with a slim chance of pinning anything down. With *Eldorado* headed for the combat zone Winthrop had more pressing duties, and the events themselves had resolved underlying problems. Instinct, Nobel held, often beat strict adherence to rules and regulations.

The morale of sailors under stress affected the performance of a ship. Thus, the Navy provided rules. For every situation confronting a man in the Navy, he could find a regulation somewhere that told him what to do. The trick was in the application.

Nobel in his years of service had seen the bad results of blind enforcement of the rules as well as loose regard for them on different vessels. And some situations demanded hiding the rule book. Johnson had proposed such a solution to the print shop striker problem.

Nobel headed to the first-class mess. He wanted Johnson's long term backing, not the superficial duty-based kind but the type of support a friend would give. Helping the second-class get Lee into Reilly's operation would cement Johnson's loyalty.

In the end the old man heard about everything that happened on his ship. If Nobel got a reputation for promoting good racial relations, it would help him win his CPO hat, and only Johnson would run the risk of being seen as promoting fights, not Nobel. *Well maybe Bode and Johnson.*

An unofficial fist fight might fix things for Mayer, and straighten out Sullivan, putting him out of the running to become a lithographer.

~

Johnson

Twirling his boatswain's pipe on its lanyard while standing at his perch on the bridge, Johnson watched Nobel and Bode as they checked the guy wires holding the admiral's barge. *He's asking Bode. He better not clue him in to what we're planning.*

If Sullivan got in a fight, he might get captain's mast. Even if he wasn't put on report, the officers wouldn't let him strike for the print shop. Brawlers stayed in deck division in Johnson's experience. Nobel was an example.

Slim's too cool to get caught in a fight himself. Johnson liked the image of his nickname, *Slim.* "Don't mess with Slim," the guys said. He fingered his sheathed razor while appearing to scratch his back.

Johnson stayed in deck department because he liked the work and was smart enough to make rank in a hurry. He assumed the white officers would approve a black man for the print shop as long as no white sailor appeared qualified. With Sullivan in trouble for fighting, Lee's background and qualifications would give the officers no reason to block him.

Johnson's take on Winthrop put the young JG in the category of a college boy acting the way he assumed an officer should act. The real Winthrop hid under the silver bars somewhere, untested, shallow, not like Johnson.

Try grown' up in the Detroit projects. Well, he worked for worse in the past.

Winthrop backed Lee for Reilly's slot because that was what an officer did, not because he trusted in him. Johnson had faith in Lee, a big difference. Still, Winthrop's backing remained key. The way to handle him: make Lee's transfer to printing something an officer would do.

159

~

Mayer

"Hey, Mayer," Sullivan said. "You get a letter from your folks in Subic?"

"Fuck you, Sullivan." Mayer continued with his tray to the table with Lee, Bode, and some other guys from first division.

"What's that all about?" Bode said.

"He's a bastard." Mayer said, eyes filling as he sat across from him.

Johnson, sitting with his regular buddies at another table, observed, turned and gave another black seaman a look. The seaman, from Roxbury, Massachusetts, hated Sullivan.

Sullivan, hailing from South Boston, harbored all the same resentment felt by his fellow Irish toward court-ordered forced busing. His animosity toward the politically motivated federal court that ordered certain Boston schools desegregated bubbled out now and then against black sailors.

The sailor's deep resentment of black Bostonians being helped at the expense of the Irish had motivated his actions in Okinawa. But Johnson's Roxbury buddies and a few other black sailors had put the fear of God in him, so Sully, as his buddies called him, backed off his racist comments and turned his hate on Mayer: "Weasel" the sneak thief. Sullivan's frustrated anger at blacks had begun to focus on Mayer when Mayer stood up for Lee at the Dragon's Breath Tavern.

Johnson saw to it that Sullivan heard about Mayer tearing up at the EM club in Taipei when he talked about his mom or dad. So the Irish sailor started on Mayer's parents.

160

Mayer had begun to notice. *Lee knew. Should he explain it to* *Bode*?

22

One evening during the Beau Charger/Belt Tight operations Winthrop was called to the bridge for the underway replenishment detail. The delicate maneuver called an UNREP involved *Eldorado* approaching the supply ship USS *Vega,* from the stern, pulling alongside at standard speed, matching her exact speed once alongside, shooting a line to *Vega*, and using that to haul a steel cable across the water. The cable was hooked to a winch system to give it sufficient tension as the space between the vessels varied. Another winch operated a line strung to a trolley that rode the cable high line and carried a load of supplies in a cargo net suspended beneath it.

The operation took place at night to avoid NVA eyes as much as possible. Knowledge of the flagship's replenishment at sea allowed the enemy to help predict future attacks. The brass added an additional level of secrecy by mandating the ships be darkened with the exception of the red and green running lights which were dimmed to 2,000-yard visibility. Red spotlights arranged on the forward well deck gave the men some visibility without ruining their night vision or highlighting *Eldorado*'s position to other vessels.

Winthrop's job on such details involved anything the captain wanted him to do. He served as an extra officer on the bridge. An UNREP operation depended on experienced hands at all stations. The chief quartermaster on *Eldorado* handled the helm, Joe Trucker stood in as OOD. On the forward well deck where the rig was set up, BM First Class Nobel bossed the work crew. The chief engineer joined the regular crew in the engine room. Hospital corpsmen and the ship's doctor stood nearby.

Still, even with the best team on watch, dangerous hazards abounded. Winthrop believed this risky maneuver should be done in daylight. He doubted the limited knowledge the NVA might derive from observing the replenishment was worth the risk at night. Perhaps the Navy regarded the situation as a training opportunity.

The strategic logic of the US activity in Vietnam escaped Winthrop. All the unnecessary risks taken with the lives young men serving their country Winthrop laid on the misinformed and haphazard policy of Lyndon Johnson who started the war in the first place.

The SEATO treaty of the fifties obligated the US to support Vietnam. But it took an act of war to get the public behind a real effort. Before Johnson's Gulf of Tonkin Resolution, based on an unsuccessful attack on a US destroyer, the US screwed around in country with advisors. The few brave green berets were insufficient to help the South Vietnamese field effective fighters. If the president assumed using the so-called sea attack to garner political backing for an all-out war effort worth the risk, his method of running the conflict after the congressional resolution showed the flaw in civilian control of the military—dumb leadership.

Naïve youngsters protested the war out of fear of being drafted, yet turned their protests against the troops, calling them baby killers. The protestors raged against bombing the enemy at its core, unrealistically ignoring the fact that their countrymen were dying because the US failed to use all its weapons, crazy.

And Johnson dithered.

Winthrop tried thinking of Mary to get his mind off the stupid commander-in-chief.

A whipping sound forward marked the first load as it zipped over the gap between ships. From Winthrop's vantage a dark form rocketed to the end of *Eldorado*'s boom. Shadowy shapes grabbed it and unhooked the cargo. A congo line of sailors, visible as silhouettes in the red glow formed and passed individual boxes of stores below decks as the now empty cargo net whisked back across the black water to the supply ship.

~

Mayer

Mayer passed another box back to Sullivan on the dark well deck, giving it an extra push as the second division sailor took it.

"Fuck you, Mayer. Your mother's a whore."

"What's your problem?" Mayer hissed.

Sullivan shoved him. "Stay outta my way, fucker."

Mayer stumbled into the sailor ahead of him who reached out and grabbed the unloaded cargo net for support.

At that moment the winch hauled the empty net back toward the *Vega* catching the sailor's fingers in a corner of the nylon webbing. He screamed and clutched his hand.

"God, sorry man," Mayer said. Then shouted, "Medic, medic, over here."

~

Winthrop noticed a commotion on the deck forward. Seamen in the congo line slowed. Nobel motioned to hold up. The doctor and some corpsmen ran to the UNREP station. They helped a man off the deck, through a hatch, and into the ship. The talker on the bridge told the

164

captain, "He lost a couple of fingers. The doc's bringing him back to sick bay."

The next day a chopper flew the injured man over to *Sanctuary*.

~

While *Eldorado* maintained her position near the DMZ the two Marine landing forces joined with 3rd Marine division units from the I Corps, northern section of South Vietnam. The Marines then hooked up with ARVN troops and attacked the enemy in several battles.

23

On May 24 the flagship returned to Da Nang harbor. The anchor, weigh anchor, and anchor-again-drill became routine, so routine the operations department had neglected to get an anchorage assignment from the harbor. Winthrop found himself on the radio handset peering out the wheelhouse porthole near the centerline. The captain, out on the port wing, conned the ship toward the harbor anchorage area.

A tired Winthrop stood haggard and drained from the watch schedule, his mood irate about the uselessness of sacrificing young Marines in the coastal jungles of Vietnam. Gloomy, reflecting that no one back home even knew or gave a damn about his ship's activities in Vietnam, Winthrop raised the handset and tried again to call Da Nang Control on the radio.

"Da Nang Control, Da Nang Control, this is *Eldorado*. Over."

"*Eldorado,* this is Da Nang Control. Over."

"Da Nang Control, *Eldorado* requests an anchorage assignment. Over."

"Roger, *Eldorado*. What cargo are you carrying? Over."

Winthrop dropped the arm holding the handset, his mouth opened and closed.

The captain stared in from the wing.

Winthrop raised the handset.

"Da Nang Control, this is *Eldorado*, I say again, request an anchorage assignment, over."

We're not a damn merchant ship.

"Roger *Eldorado*. Interrogative, what cargo are you carrying? Over."

All the frustration and fatigue of the whole deployment boiled over in his mind. Winthrop roared into the handset:

"Da Nang Control, this is *Eldorado*. Be advised, *Eldorado* is a man-of-war with flag embarked."

Silence reigned on the bridge. Then the old man guffawed.

Winthrop stood defiant, red faced, and pissed off.

They didn't cheer but their faces told him the bridge crew agreed.

Johnson pulled a wide grin, full of white teeth, with eyes unlidded. At that instant Johnson perceived the man beneath the silver bars.

"You tell, 'em, Mister Winthrop," he said.

Da Nang Control spoke. "Eldorado your assigned anchorage is Alfa two, three. A23."

~

All over the ship sailors talked about it at the ship's store while buying cigarettes, on the mess decks, in the CPO mess, and the first-class lounge.

When Winthrop sat in the wardroom Larsen mentioned it first. He leaned back while pulling the napkin out of his ring and said, "Man-of-war, flag embarked."

The guys chuckled.

Winthrop enjoyed celebrity status for a day or so.

Reflecting about it later, Winthrop realized he had voiced the feeling of every man on the ship. Tired of the long hours, hard work and no liberty, to a man they wondered if anyone gave a damn about what they were doing.

Eldorado was a man-of-war and she carried the flag of the commander amphibious forces Pacific Fleet.

Many merchant ships supplied the city of Da Nang as well as the large US base. It was understandable that the civil servant on the Da Nang Control radio should ask about her cargo. Even the name *Eldorado* sounded like a merchant ship.

Funny, a small thing like his response on a radio telephone could affect so many. He figured the crew of *Eldorado* was thinking the same as he at that instant. *Christ, they were Eldorado sailors and proud of it.* He said the right thing when the men needed it.

~

Standing watch at anchor bored the hell out Winthrop. The weight of the .45 around his waist added to the discomfort of the steel deck on his feet and the resulting ache that ran up his shins. But the threat from VC swimmers or even a small boat remained real. He stiffened his back, stretched, and looked around.

Johnson stood leaning near the 1 MC. With nothing to announce at 0300, the time now, he conferred with the bridge talker.

The quartermaster of the watch, out by Lee on the port wing, sighted a bearing on the Da Nang observatory light. He would mark a line from the light on the harbor chart, along with the bearing of two other landmarks, providing a firm fix. This regular routine assured no anchor slippage. The ship swung around as the tide moved in and out but stayed in its assigned area indicated by circle A23 on the chart. Sixty fathoms of chain held the old girl in seven fathoms of water.

To Winthrop's senses the full moon provided an exotic, glassy sheen on the harbor, the air's stillness marred only by the light creaking of the anchor chain. The gray deck, cool now, would pick up a coat of dew in the morning.

Peaceful, but I'd rather be sleeping.

~

Johnson

The bridge sound powered phone talker blathered on about his home town in Tennessee, trying to hold Johnson's attention. Johnson had suggested him to Nobel for the talker duty figuring to use the kid's natural tendency to like talking. He regretted the recommendation now. No matter how bored Johnson got and how often he yawned, the kid blabbed on.

Winthrop always expected him to train the black sailors, something he resented. Yet Johnson realized in some part of his brain that Winthrop was doing the same as Johnson always did, take advantage of a man's proclivities. The talker, a black guy not long out of boot camp, did receive more attention in training than most white sailors under Johnson's supervision.

"Call the sentries," he said, "so they'll be awake when Mister Larsen gets to 'em."

Relieved to get away, he strolled back to the quartermaster shack to refill his coffee. He spotted the moon. *Same moon Leticia and the kids can see.* The thought gave him comfort.

He was trying to maneuver Mayer into something that would help a black guy, Lee, and at Mayer's expense. These truths never surfaced from Johnson's unconscious, held down by his upbringing in the Detroit projects and an ingrown "us against them" mindset.

~

169

Mayer

Mayer's feet hurt. He failed to appreciate the scenic full moon reflecting on the water. His shoulder ached where the M-1's sling dug into it. The damn sound-powered phone hung around his neck with the voice microphone levered out on struts anchored to pads on his chest. The straps of the device around the back of his neck caused him to stretch out his chin every few minutes to relieve the pressure. The weight of the headphones pressed against the tops of his ears. Every quarter hour the bridge talker would come on and say, "Radio check."

"Port-quarter sentry, loud and clear," he would answer.

He began to think of a career. Bode told him he'd put him in for third-class petty officer when the next test came up. Lee told him Johnson would back him for it. He heard Winthrop would recommend most sailors for the third-class exam if they wanted to advance themselves. *I can do it.*

Larsen walked up to him. "Quiet night 'eh? Everything secure here?"

"Yes sir, but my damn feet hurt and this sound powered phone is bugging me."

Larsen patted his .45. "This damn thing is weighing on me too. Welcome to the club. We only got another hour on this watch. Carry on."

Larsen moved on and climbed the ladder out of the aft well deck and headed back to the bridge.

Mayer watched. *Wonder how you get to be an officer.*

~

On May 28 with no respite for the crew and under the admiral's orders, the old flagship weighed anchor once again and steamed fifty miles south to Chu Li, anchoring offshore from the Marine air base.

Flagship

On May 29 *Eldorado* proceeded farther south and anchored off Qui Nhon, site of an Army and an Air Force air base. She returned to Da Nang the next day.

Each time the old warship anchored and weighed anchor the special detail requirement pulled tired sailors off jobs or out of the rack. Each anchorage involved unloading boats and later, loading boats for runs to shore as well as multiple soundings of flight quarters for the coming and going of choppers. Winthrop wondered if the admiral appreciated the challenge of these special duties in addition to the one-in-three watches and routine ship's work.

Winthrop seldom saw the key man *Eldorado* housed and for whom she provided communication and transportation services. His personal quarters occupied most of the space below the bridge. The ship's crew, including officers, rarely entered the area his staff occupied immediately below his quarters. Only once or twice during the deployment did the man stroll around his veranda deck under the bridge.

All the various duties of the 450-man crew of the magnificent mechanical device called *Eldorado* served one objective: deliver the headquarters of this important man to the scene of the war.

~

The Beau Charger/Belt Tight operations wrapped up May 28. The US lost 156 sailors and Marines to the North's reported loss of 447 men. Winthrop, reading the results on the OOD message board, remained skeptical of the US tactics and the North Vietnamese body count.

From Winthrop's viewpoint, a direct all-out attack on North Vietnam after heavy bombing of military, industrial, and civilian areas would work. A massive landing of US troops in the North, leaving South Vietnam's defense to the ARV, would change the course of the war. Ho

171

Chi Min would have no choice but to surrender or watch the destruction of his country. The same could be done with nukes and no loss of American lives. Instead, the US fought on North Vietnam's terms. President Johnson didn't understand the concept. You fight all out to win. Otherwise what's the point of declaring war and sacrificing Americans?

Winthrop didn't object to his service. Unlike the war protestors, he believed that he owed his service to his country. In a world where the jungle law prevailed, if a country didn't have a military to protect the homeland, the homeland would not long endure. Vietnam existed far from the homeland but the "war of liberation" there was a model for future world conquest by the communist ideology.

Like many his age, he felt like a cork adrift on a vast sea of government incompetence. Winthrop believed in duty, honor, and country, but his shipmates received his main loyalty. His directed his chief frustration at the president.

At his core Winthrop's personal honor depended upon his loyal service. If he died he would enter eternal life, or if there was no God at least there would be no more pain and his family would honor him. *You have to have values, or what's the point?*

Best not to think it to death, Fred. You get nowhere doing that. Your mind goes around and around in an unsolvable loop of philosophy. Just do your duty. Things will take care of themselves.

24

Giving the Marines no break, the task force landed SLF Alpha on June 2. Storming ashore in a conventional seaborne and airborne assault about twenty-five miles south of the DMZ, the Alpha force kicked off operation Bear Bite while *Eldorado* remained farther south in Da Nang harbor.

On June 4 Winthrop took over the bridge watch for the eight-to-twelve at 0730, as the convention dictated, so the early morning watch could get some breakfast. After walking around reviewing the situation, he checked the chart and the ship's various fixes as she swung in the anchorage. He found no indication of anchor dragging. The air carried a slight smell of sewage blowing from land. The morning sun brightened the clear sky. His charge for the next four hours floated in the middle of a war zone, secure because her crew did their jobs.

He walked to the port side where he heard men talking. Six men about his age, hard, fit, serious, and wearing camouflage uniforms, stood on the quarterdeck. Deposited by a boat crew from Da Nang a few minutes earlier, they carried M-16s and back-packs and talked with a commander on the admiral's staff.

The chief quartermaster ambled up to Winthrop.

"SEAL team," he said. "Admiral's got 'em doing something."

"Oh I thought they might be UDT."

"Same difference. Now the Navy calls them SEALS. Still do underwater demolition work, but now their job involves all sorts of commando stuff."

The SEALS went inside.

173

"Quartered with the admiral's staff," the chief said. "I think we're taking them somewhere."

Winthrop's father, retired Navy himself, told Winthrop as he headed off to OCS, "Stay away from the UDT. Leave that to the glory boys." That was barely two years before.

Winthrop took his father's advice, didn't volunteer. He looked at the commandos. Not *glory boys*, he thought. His service experience tipped his feelings away from the old man's advice. Sure, his father wanted him to come home alive. But these were not glory boys. The requirements of their jobs ran far too dangerous for that flippant description. They were the best the country had.

At 1500 *Eldorado* weighed anchor. At dusk the word came on the 1 MC. "Now darken ship, darken ship, dim navigation lights." He took the first night watch, the 2000-to-2400 watch. No interior lights shown from the flagship. Outside, only her dimmed port and starboard running lights shown, making them visible for 2,000 yards at the most, and she extinguished her white masthead lights and stern light. Winthrop allowed his eyes to adjust. When he could distinguish things in the wheelhouse under only the glow from the radar repeater and the dim red light over the chart table, he relieved Jay Dunston.

"Where we headed?" he asked Dunston.

"Don't know. Orders give us a southern heading, course one nine zero."

Dunston pointed to a ledger on the chart table.

"The captain's night orders say keep our speed at ten knots and continue until the flag watch officer advises us."

Winthrop kept the ship on one nine zero until Tom Reynolds relieved him at midnight. Sometime in the early morning hours, as

174

Flagship

Winthrop slept, *Eldorado* slowed and stopped. The SEAL team disembarked on a rubber raft. Winthrop never learned their objective, the outcome of their mission, nor would the majority of the Navy, and none of their countrymen. That's how they operated.

The flagship continued south to Na Trang, headquarters for US Air Force commandos, and anchored on June 5. Helicopters came and went. Winthrop, with no idea what the flag was up to, stuck to doing his job—"do your job," the watchword for lower-level servicemen of all ranks and ratings. Men did their duty, trusting in their superiors.

~

Early evening found *Eldorado* underway once again. She arrived in the morning of June 6 at Cam Ranh Bay, not far south of Na Trang. When the sea and anchor detail finished, the old girl floated at anchor a short boat ride off the beach from the base for fast patrol craft, or PCFs, known as swift boats.

An announcement came on the 1MC: "Liberty will be allowed for one-half the crew from 1200 to 1400 and the other half from 1400 to 1600."

Before this, the crew had enjoyed no liberty in Vietnam. Only officers in the admiral's complement went ashore for any period of time. Winthrop suspected not all those staff trips concerned business.

The unsophisticated PCF base included one large quonset hut which served as a community tavern. No one complained about the dusty walk from the swift boat pier to the bar and beach area. Some sailors headed to the beach to swim but most ended at the bar.

Winthrop joined the first liberty party and walked to the saloon on the primitive base. The place accepted officers and enlisted men without restrictions. The men left most divisions of rank on the ship and mingled freely.

The crude structure's furniture, salvaged from clubs at bases around Asia, served their purpose. The drab, light green walls and scratches and grime from past parties deterred no one. Four-by-fours supported the steel-plate covered bar which ran the long way across one side of the hut. Winthrop figured Seabees built it for the swifties. Officers and men clambered inside, grabbed seats, and ordered beer, the only alcoholic beverage available.

Forty-five minutes for the liberty boat round-trip and the walk to the place left an hour to drink one's fill and enjoy the beach. Most crewmen opted to drink the only beer brand available, San Miguel. The stuff came from the Philippines but enjoyed a near monopoly among troops in certain areas of Vietnam. Legend told of Marines halting a fire-fight raging across a river so the beer boat could pass.

As Winthrop entered the bar Johnson waved him over to an open stool.

"Not much time," Johnson said. "And the beer choice isn't much."

Winthrop grinned, thinking those were the most words Johnson ever said to him.

"We'll make the best of it, Slim."

~

Johnson

"First time ya ever called me Slim, Mister W."

Hobnobbing with white officers. Wait till Leticia hears about this.

"Two beers over here," Winthrop said to the bartender.

They clinked bottles.

"Any word on my man Lee?" Johnson said.

176

"Reilly was gonna pick Sully," Winthrop said, "but since Lee applied, he kicked the decision up to Mister Edger. Now Edger's off the ship and the XO doesn't want any personnel changes till we're headed back to the States."

Winthrop shrugged. "I like Lee. He's a smart sailor and upbeat. Hope he gets the job."

"Hope so too." Johnson hoisted his bottle, taking a long pull.

"*Mount McKinley*'s due end of this month," Winthrop said. "Should know soon."

"Thanks, Mister W. Gotta join some of my buddies."

He maneuvered past Winthrop toward a group of black petty officers.

~

Mayer

Bode and Lee waived Mayer over to their table when he walked in.

"Over here, man."

They held San Miguels in hand.

"What took ya?" Bode said.

"Stopped to look at one of those Swifties. Maybe I'll volunteer."

"Good way to make rank," Bode said. "Also a good way to die."

"Johnson says the brown water Navy ain't so cool," Lee said. "*Eldorado*'s a good feeder too. Why give up the good chow for C-Rations?"

"You'll make lithographer third pretty soon after you get in the print shop," Mayer said. "I got a lotta gigs on my record. Gotta do it the hard way. Anyway that'll get me away from that bastard Sullivan."

177

"There are Sullivans all over," Bode said. "Just stand up to him like you been, he'll go away."

"I might just punch him in the face next time he mouths off."

"What's the deal about your parents?" Bode said. "Why's he always ragging on you about them?"

Mayer looked at Lee, sighed. "Pop went missing at Normandy. Mom don't believe it, still." His eyes filled. "Sorry can't hardly talk about it." He hesitated. "Well Mom's turned into a drunk."

"Sully know that?" Bode said.

"No one knew that 'till now, but someone told him how I feel."

"Not me," Lee said.

~

Nobel

Nobel joined the second liberty party with Hoffman of second division. They sat at the bar sipping San Miguels.

"Hear anything 'bout your CPO hat?" Hoffman said.

"Naw, nothing," Nobel said." Maybe after we get to the States."

"Hope ya do. *Mount Mac*'s coming to relieve us next month."

"So I hear. I'll probably retire with twenty if I don't get chief."

"That pension ain't much."

"Enough in Caribou. I'll sell firewood in the fall and plow driveways in the winter if I need extra cash."

"How about spring and summer?"

"Trout fishin'."

Commander Webster pushed his way in-between. "Got room here for another old fart?"

"Sure, Commander, you buyin'?" Nobel said.

"That the fishin' you're talking about?" The XO grinned.

178

25

After the last liberty boat returned from the swift boat base *Eldorado* weighed anchor and steamed to Vung Tau, a large city on the northern edge of the Mekong Delta. Winthrop supposed the admiral planned some sort of meeting with the 1st Australian Logistical Support Group in Vietnam which headquartered there.

Winthrop conned the old girl to its Vung Tau anchorage on June 7. The same drill prevailed: waterline lights and a picket boat at night, and armed sentries on the weather decks at all times. Helicopters came and went.

The four-to-eight morning watch June 8 started quiet but proved a trying one for Winthrop. About 0500 he got a call from the combat information center.

"Conn, Combat," the 21MC squawked. "We got many contacts coming our way from the shore."

Winthrop rushed over to the intercom box, pushed the CIC button, and pulled down the talk lever.

"Combat, can you identify them?"

"Not yet."

Winthrop jogged over to the starboard side which faced land, and put his binoculars in that direction. Predawn light started to filter over the horizon in the eastern sky. He viewed small dark shapes, nothing else.

He hustled back to the wheelhouse and punched the button for the signal bridge.

179

"Signal Bridge, Conn, challenge those contacts off to starboard."

"Signal Bridge, aye."

Then, "Conn, Signal Bridge, No response from those contacts."

Put the ship at General Quarters?

He tried one more thing. He picked up the radio handset in the wheelhouse and called Vung Tau harbor control on the administrative net.

"Vung Tau Control, this is *Eldorado,* over."

"*Eldorado*, this is Vung Tau Control, over."

"We got many contacts approaching us. Can you identify?"

"Roger *Eldorado*, that's the fishing fleet going out this morning."

Winthrop hit the 21MC lever for CIC again.

"Combat, bridge, thanks for the heads up. The contacts are the Vung Tau fishing fleet for your info."

Tense sailors on the bridge overheard and relaxed.

The 21MC squawked again.

"Conn, Signal Bridge, those contacts appear to be fishing boats."

~

Later in the day the ship received the news about an attack on another US ship. An embattled Israel accidentally damaged the USS *Liberty,* a spy ship operating in the Mediterranean and monitoring the Six Day War in the Middle East. In a screw-up Israel failed to identify its American ally.

Winthrop had avoided the same mistake that morning.

The following day *Eldorado* moved further south and anchored off shore from the swift boat base on the tiny island of An Thoi located off the coast of Cambodia and the southernmost possession of South Vietnam.

~

Mayer

"Johnson says he can arrange a fight between you and Sullivan," Lee said.

Mayer had finished his 2000-to-2400 watch and sat in the crews mess enjoying *midrats* with Lee and Bode. He munched a hamburger and sipped a Pepsi.

"A fight? I'd like to punch him out, but I don't need captain's mast."

"How's Johnson gonna do that?" Bode said.

"Oh, a couple senior boatswain's mates can supervise it," Lee said. "Keep you from killing each other. He says we can use auto storage. Nobody goes down there. The old man won't find out."

Mayer swallowed.

"Sullivan know this?"

"Not yet."

"Maybe I'll just haul off and cold-cock him. That would fix him. No formalities of a supervised fist fight."

"Screw Sully, got some good news guys," Bode said, "The chicks are world class in Bangkok and we're headed there tomorrow. What say the three of us make liberty together?"

"Chicks like in Olongapo?" Lee said.

"Better, like Taiwan, and I remember the right places."

"Sign us up," Mayer said.

~

Johnson

After sea and anchor detail on June 9, Johnson approached Nobel.

"Buy ya coffee on the mess decks."

181

They got their coffee and sat at one of the steel tables.

"Can you get a small group into auto storage?" Johnson said.

"Shouldn't be down there while underway, the vehicles are stored there."

"Yeah but they're tied down. We left the admiral's Lincoln back in Subic. Mayer and Sullivan can fight in the empty space."

Nobel took a long sip of his coffee, savored it, frowned, and moved around on his seat.

"Look, I asked Bode to buddy up with Mayer and Lee, don't ask me to have anything to do with this."

"No one has to know except a couple of boatswains mates . . . and Reilly."

"And what if an officer finds out?"

"None will."

"To get down there you got to open a condition X-ray hatch. Shouldn't be opened when underway."

"God damn it, Nobel. We'll do it when we get to Subic then."

~

Nobel

Nobel didn't like it.

Johnson's plan sounds like a damn soap opera scheme. Better talk to Winthrop.

Nobel wandered into the deck office and checked his box. He picked up a corrected correspondence course for Mayer—"Boatswains Mate Third-Class"—and a note from Winthrop asking him to check the stay on the port boom.

Distracted by Johnson's scheme, he knocked against LTJG Randolph who sat reading *All Hands* magazine.

182

Randolph looked up.

"Oh, Nobel, my first-class tells me Johnson's goin' around promoting a fight between your sailor Mayer, and Sullivan in my division. You know anything 'bout that?"

"Huh, no sir."

Words out. Now what am I gonna do?"

~

From An Thoi, *Eldorado* steamed about 350 miles Northwest in the Gulf of Thailand to the entrance of Bangkok Harbor. Formed by a river, the geography of the harbor necessitated that vessels enter along a ship channel cut through a permanent alluvial sand bar with a depth of six to twelve feet depending on the tide.

Pulling a draft of about twenty-eight feet *Eldorado* timed her arrival at the bar to high tide. The harbor pilot met her there and Winthrop gave up the conn to him and Captain Ridgeway. Dredged, the entrance channel to Bangkok ran only twenty-six to twenty-eight feet deep, thirty feet at high tide.

Winthrop's position as sea and anchor detail OOD provided him a post with a view of the tropical Shangri-La. As the harbor pilot and the captain conned *Eldorado* through the bar and along the river channel, Winthrop enjoyed golden temple spires levitating over the morning mist-covered water on both sides of the ship.

Only the stifling heat and humidity marred the arrival experience until an owl landed in the row of life rafts stowed on the port side. The old man didn't like the incident. He conferred with the Thai harbor pilot.

The buzz on the bridge: In Thailand an owl landing on a building was a bad omen. The pilot agreed with the captain, the omen applied to a ship.

183

Captain Ridgway called his steward out to the bridge. The man left and returned with Ridgway's .22-caliber rifle. He fired two shots before the bird fell.

Brutal, arrogant, unnecessary . . . or timely, do four-stripers study psychology as a prerequisite for command, Winthrop wondered? Reports of the strange occurrence circulated the ship. The scuttlebutt about the captain's action gave him a certain macho status. The crew always respected him. Along with the respect now came a bit of fear. He became bigger than life, fabled perhaps. Any veteran who has ever served on a ship likes to recount a personal experience or two with the ship's captain. The position itself creates a certain mythos. At sea the old man is God.

Winthrop wondered if Ridgway shot the bird on purpose to create a distraction for a crew whose long hours of work at sea may have generated certain frictions which the old man didn't want acted out on liberty. Without doubt the owl didn't plan to alight on the ship.

The crew existed as a living thing in its own right, greater than its parts. Landlubbers understood the concept of calling a ship a lady. She existed as a hunk of steel until a crew manned her, maintained her, prettied her up, and then she took on a persona of her own.

What landlubbers didn't understand was the crew developed a persona which transcended the ship herself. The persona changed over time because of its intimate relation to the ethereal thing called morale. The individual crew members went about their lives with their own concerns, unrelated to each other. Yet, at times, like a school of fish, they moved in unison as if an invisible web connected them. That phenomenon had happened the day he informed Da Nang control *Eldorado* was a man-of-war with flag embarked. Knowledge of the event raced through the crew. It happened once more when the old man shot the owl.

184

The crew, to a man, identified as *Eldorado* sailors. They walked a little taller. *Their captain shot an owl off the port life rafts.*

~

Did the owl represent an omen? Winthrop was not superstitious but the thought bugged him.

~

The four-day break allowed the whole crew time on the beach in the exotic port where souvenirs, scrumptious food, and sensual delights abounded.

A funk followed Winthrop as he made liberty with Dunston and the guys. His last letter from Mary sounded a bit ambiguous and with his current absence, her image seemed to fade. His thoughts moved to his own position. He wasn't married but bore an obligatory restraint from seeking female companionship. Rendered impotent in the romance game, his Navy assignment requiring hours of service as a watch officer, a ship driver some might say, left him in a similar fuzzy position as to his future occupation. How many ship handlers where there in the business world?

Bangkok's claim to fame with sailors wasn't the cheap hotel rooms and bar girls like those of Olongapo, or the exotic, first-class love making available in Taiwan. Beautiful Thai girls abounded in clean, glitzy massage parlors. The places offered the traditional bath and massage, plus the exotic feel of a lithe young woman's bare feet on one's back. When the service reached that point and a scanty clad girl climbed on a guy's back the sailor underwent a thrill worthy of writing home about. And thus he could describe a glamorous experience without once mentioning the final happy ending involving the girl's silken hand strokes. And most of the young women would, for an extra fee, accept an assignation in a close by hotel.

185

Winthrop skipped the girls, and each day of liberty he and Dunston returned to the ship loaded with overpriced souvenirs and less-than-upbeat-dispositions.

Winthrop's personal mood notwithstanding, a rested and happy crew sailed for Vietnam June 16.

26

On June 19, the thirteen bongs followed by "General quarters, general quarters, all hands man their battle stations," sounding over the 1MC did not fail to cause Winthrop's heart to beat hard. Now the ninth time his shipmates had manned battle stations on this deployment, the call to action raised the same excited anticipation as the first time. Like his fellow crewmembers he didn't know what awaited him on his station.

SLF Alpha Marines got the call for Operation Beacon Torch. From Winthrop's perch on the bridge he watched waves of choppers leave *Tripoli,* an amphibious assault helicopter carrier.

The air assault landing hit quick and hard. The choppers dropped the brave Marines in landing zones Cardinal and Wren near Hoi An. A tank battalion and the rest of the force landed on Red Beach, a designated seaborne landing zone. After some confusion caused by errors in hitting the chopper landing zones, Alpha engaged about 100 NVA regulars in pitched battle.

Kitty Hawk, providing air cover for the fighting Marines, steamed in the area, along with *Eldorado, Tripoli,* and *Clarion County*, an old landing ship converted to fire rockets.

After general quarters, the operation proceeded in a routine fashion for Winthrop, but night watches still challenged him. Most nights when the messenger-of-the-watch roused him for his turn on the bridge, he woke in a confident mood. But fatigue stalked him and some nights, as he sat in the wardroom with a wake-up cup of coffee, fear found a home in the recesses of his mind.

One such watch occurred during the Beacon Torch operation. The rotation put Winthrop on the four-to-eight that morning. Miscellaneous muffled grinds and groans resonated as low background noise throughout the ship as he showered, dressed, and headed to the wardroom—sounds of a maneuvering ship. Jay Dunston had his hands full on the bridge.

As the fog in his head lifted while he sipped coffee, fear rose up to replace it. The abrupt sensation appeared much like the first rays of sunlight bursting over the horizon at sea, focused, hard. In minutes he would replace Jay on the bridge maneuvering a 12,000 ton ship, home to 550 souls, at night, at darken ship, in the combat zone. He fiddled with the anchor and shield device of his piss-cutter hat lying on the table and wondered what other men his age in the States were doing.

Larsen joined him for coffee. No longer full of naive self-confident bravado of his early months on *Eldorado*, Larsen sat with a tired sigh.

"Gonna be a bugger."

"Tell me about it," Winthrop said.

They downed their coffee in silence. Winthrop picked up his hat. "We better get up there."

~

Dunston, his overseas cap wilted on his head, the faint smell of BO emanating from his body, bent over the chart table completing his log.

He straightened. "Better brief you," he said.

In the darkness he led Winthrop to the radar repeater. As Winthrop followed, his eyes not yet adjusted to the blackness, he stumbled on the helmsman's platform. The two officers leaned over the dimmed radar repeater. Its sweep lit up several contacts. Dunston's grease pencil markings labeled them: *Clarion River,* the rocket ship; *Tripoli,* the helo carrier; and *Kitty Hawk,* the attack carrier.

"Kitty Hawk's close, about 2,000 yards, but she's opening," he said. "Those three fishing boats . . ." He indicated three blips he had marked "FB" on the radar . . . "I challenged them, no response, but the signal bridge says they're fishing boats. They put the big glasses on 'em. The boats came pretty close a few minutes ago, but they're headed out to open ocean."

He pointed out *Eldorado's* night steaming area, drawn on the radar in the form of a rectangle, about five miles wide and ten miles long. The captain's night orders directed OODs to steam in the indicated zone on various courses and at various speeds. The screen showed that his ship approached the northern edge of the defined area. He needed to turn south. *Clarion River* operated about four miles to the southeast. *Tripoli* loitered to the north and closer to the coast than *Kitty Hawk* which loomed nearby off the starboard bow.

Larsen relieved his counterpart and strode out to the starboard wing, near the lookout. Winthrop and Dunston walked back to the chart table on the port side of the wheelhouse.

With a sigh, Winthrop placed his empty coffee cup on the chart table. Other watch standers relieved their counterparts. Dunston signed his deck log, handed Winthrop the challenge code device, saluted.

Returning the salute, Winthrop followed protocol and said, "I relieve you, sir."

Larsen called him to the starboard wing, urgency in his voice, "Fred, take a look at this. *Kitty Hawk*'s on a steady bearing."

Yawning, Winthrop stepped up on the pelorus and sighted an obscure shape twenty-one degrees off the bow. The bearing stayed the same for the minute he stood there.

189

When a ship continues on a steady bearing the key information a ship handler needs is the range. If the range gets longer, fine, the vessel is moving away, but if the range is closing, a collision will occur unless one of the ships maneuvers.

She's opening.

Winthrop remembered Dunston's comment about the huge vessel. He put his binoculars on the carrier. A dim red light glowed from the otherwise black hulk off Eldorado's starboard bow.

When a vessel's night operations called for darken ship with dim navigation running lights, as they did now, only dim red for port and dim green for starboard lights showed. The dimmed setting allowed only 2,000 yards visibility. Built-in blinders shielded the two running lights profiles to the forward 112.5 degrees of the hull. Therefore, an OOD viewing no lights knew his vessel approached a radar contact from somewhere astern, or more than one nautical mile away. If he observed a red light, he closed from the port side less than a nautical mile away. The darkened ship, dim navigation mode, rendered the visual estimate of a contact's aspect and her course, tricky.

The single red light in Winthrop's binoculars told him *Kitty Hawk* was crossing from right to left. Like two cars coming to an intersection, the two ships would collide if they continued without stopping. The ships were not opening as Dunston had said.

The sea lacked roads and stop signs but nations set protocols, *the maritime rules of the road.* Consistent with the maritime rules, Winthrop's obligation called for a turn to his right, hence turning to pass astern of *Kitty Hawk*. Instead of passing behind the carrier, however, he planned to continue to the right until on a course headed south. The track would take him around to a reciprocal course in his steaming area, allowing him ten miles before his next turn. The whole maneuver was routine.

Only one other possible source of a red light in the darken ship, dim navigation lights environment existed, a red spotlight shining on a fueling station. How would one reckon the odds of a carrier refueling while underway at night, at darken ship? And how would one reckon the odds an oil tanker steaming alongside the carrier, its own green starboard running light covered in grime, would block out the carrier's starboard running light? And how would one reckon the odds that the red spotlight would show through the oiler's superstructure in a way which appeared in Winthrop's mind as the carrier's port running light? And how would one reckon the odds a competent OOD, Jay Dunston, would tell his relief that a contact closing on a collision course was *opening?*

It all happened. And it all happened on Winthrop's watch that night.

"Right standard rudder," Winthrop said.

"Right standard rudder, aye," the helmsman answered.

Then, "Rudder is right standard, sir."

In the seconds preceding the ship's response to the rudder Winthrop walked out to the starboard wing, his eye on the vague hulk off the bow. Larsen stood farther outboard, his glasses on the carrier.

Winthrop felt his ship begin to turn to port.

As the energy of the turn became clear, the carrier lit up, her full underway lighting system on bright. Stunned, Winthrop froze, staring, as he faced an image that scorched his consciousness. He rushed toward the helm as the radio sounded:

"*Eldorado, Eldorado!* My Romeo Corpin One-eight-zero."

Christ!

191

Her lights confirmed her course and status—red over white over red on her masthead meaning restricted maneuvering and Romeo Corpin meant "replenishment course" as defined in the international signal book.

If he continued the turn to starboard *Eldorado* would collide with *Kitty Hawk* and an oil tanker, steaming south, a fuel hose strung between the two. The two ships had been tracking to pass close down his port side.

I'm turning right damn in front of them.

His mind raced. The lost steerage incident in the San Bernardino Straights came rushing up to his conscious mind. *Can't go to hard left, may lose the rudder.*

"Left full rudder," he shouted.

"Left full rudder, aye, aye, sir." The helmsman barked.

Johnson, boatswain's mate of the watch, alert, moved behind the helmsman, the most critical man at the moment.

The engine can goose the turn.

"All ahead flank," Winthrop thundered.

"All ahead flank, aye, aye, sir." The engine room talker shouted and rang it up on the engine order telegraph.

And Johnson was there, backing up.

"Engine room acknowledges, all ahead flank, sir."

Grabbing the flange, Winthrop hung to the hatch between the wheelhouse and the starboard wing of the bridge.

"Rudder is left full, sir." The cry came from the helm.

Eldorado shuddered as her bow continued turning right, her 12,000 tons of momentum straining against the new rudder angle. Winthrop stared, stopped breathing, the wheelhouse went silent. The engine room guys needed to add a third burner on both boilers to gin up enough steam pressure for flank speed.

Might not help. Might be too late. The engine room crew must be frantic.

The crisis came at the worst time: as watches changed. Sleepy men trying to get oriented hit with an emergency, a critical task. OODs did not call for flank speed for drill, the crew, Winthrop figured, must know their ship, their home, faced an imminent threat.

Kitty Hawk, navigation lights ablaze, closed. Winthrop released his grip on the hatch, joined Larsen on the wing. They stared at the bow as if their sheer will would make it start moving to the left.

Seconds ticked off like hours in a slow-moving hourglass. The bow stopped progressing right. For an instant, as if time suspended itself, the bow froze, aimed at the two ships bound together by the oil line.

The scenario Winthrop feared now was the carrier initiating an emergency break away leaving the oiler to take the potential hit. He considered sounding two short whistle blasts so the other ships' crews would know that he ordered his own rudder left. As he moved toward *Eldorado's* whistle he calculated the potential. *They can see us, a whistle might confuse things.*

Cool heads prevailed on *Kitty Hawk*. The two ships continued steady-on. *Eldorado's* bow, visible to the two ships, began to turn to port.

Thank God.

Larsen and Winthrop stood rooted for seconds until Winthrop trotted across the bridge forward of the wheelhouse to the port wing. He needed a visual check of the water ahead as his ship turned. His mental picture based on his earlier review of the radar screen told him *Tripoli* should be clear and far off the port bow. His eyes confirmed a dark hulk in

193

that direction. And *Clarion River* should be invisible, as *Eldorado* came about, being far off and closer to shore.

It was over.

"All ahead two-thirds," he ordered, poking his head in the wheelhouse.

"Aye, aye, sir, all ahead two-thirds." The talker rang it up on the engine order telegraph.

Then, "Engine room acknowledges all ahead two-thirds, sir."

Those poor bastards down in that inferno of an engine room can relax now.

"Continue left to course one-nine-zero," Winthrop instructed the helm.

"One-nine-zero, aye, sir," the helmsman acknowledged.

Larsen joined him. "They went back to darken ship," he said. "Guess there's no point in calling the captain."

"What could he do now?" Winthrop frowned, rolled his eyes, and shook his head. *What would you have done, Larsen?*

"No, no, I mean . . .," Larsen said, "just . . . well . . . sometimes standard protocol . . . well, you know."

Concurring, he patted Larsen on the shoulder.

"Yeah, sorry. Too late now."

He hadn't called the captain. Had he blown the whistle, the captain would have been on the bridge like a shot. Would that have helped? No. Call him now? It's four-fifteen in the morning.

"Course, if I call him now, what am I supposed to say? 'Captain, I almost collided with *Kitty Hawk.*'"

Winthrop walked over to the chart table and examined the quartermaster log. All his commands to the helm and engine room had been recorded meticulously. The watch quartermaster had done his job. Winthrop's own log would only report actual course changes, not the orders to the helm. The ship had been running at eight knots when he assumed the watch. His log would only record the speed he reached after calling for flank speed and then back to two-thirds or eight knots. He debated changing the OOD log protocol and inserting all his orders to the helm.

Both logs were legal records and important in a court of inquiry had a collision occurred and had they survived. Like all such logs they were destined to be housed in the national archives. He decided orders to the helm belonged properly in the quartermaster log, not the deck log.

Winthrop had no further obligation to explain this event. Yet his mind would never be at ease about it. Could he have done something different? Yes, if CIC were running the dead reckoning tracer, the DRT, and if he had stopped in the combat information center before his watch to look at the situation, he would have known *Kitty Hawk*'s course and speed and the fact that it was unrepping. He had checked the radar men's picture before his watch in the past, but it wasn't a required protocol and CIC rarely had the DRT up and running.

But Dunston, why didn't he know? If his watch ran a few minutes later . . .

Had there been a collision the logs would prove Winthrop's fault irrefutably. He turned into the two ships, violating the rules of the road. The surreal coincidences that lead to his decision would be irrelevant. The captain would hang higher than Winthrop for not maintaining an effective CIC watch and for appointing Winthrop as an officer of the deck in the first place.

His imagination created mirages of the truth. His ship was under orders for dim navigation lights. What if the orders to the carrier and the oiler called for *full* darken ship? That too would explain no running lights visible and only the refueling station red spotlight showing. His mind latched onto the idea. Certainly *Kitty Hawk* took orders from the commander of the Pacific Fleet. *Eldorado's* admiral commanded only the amphibious forces of the fleet. Maybe there was a screw-up in coordinating night steaming orders from the two commands.

He pictured briefly an article in *Naval Institute Proceedings* titled, "The Hazards of Darken Ship Replenishment at Sea," citing his experience. He would receive a letter of commendation for exposing the risk of the UNREP red spotlight being mistaken for a port running light.

Forget it, Winthrop. You screwed up.

27

"You two look pale this mornin'," Chips Beasley announced as Winthrop and Larsen walked into the wardroom and slouched at their table.

"I had the watch in the engine room," he said. "You called for flank speed. What happened?"

Winthrop explained.

"Christ, I thought she was opening," Dunston said. "Sorry . . . Those damn fishing boats. I shoulda watched *Kitty Hawk* closer."

Because of the near tragedy Winthrop discovered something about individuals confronting an extreme threat. His past life had not flashed before his eyes. He had not thought of his parents. He had not thought of Mary. Only the immediate risk of catastrophe held his focus. Was it training, experience? He had logged many hours conning the ship.

He didn't freeze, he acted. That he attributed to his own psyche.

Now as his shipmates discussed the incident his mind went to his folks, and Mary. What would they do and how would they deal with their own future had the catastrophe occurred? Winthrop's head filled with the enormity of the potential scenario, a collision with a carrier loaded with aviation fuel and bombs of all description, and a supply ship carrying tons of fuel oil in her tanks, as many as 6,000 men in the three ships. The picture rushed through him like the wash from a tsunami.

Chips was talking, ". . . so when I hear 'all ahead flank' rung up on the engine order telegraph, I know the OOD is in trouble up there."

"You musta shit," Larsen said.

"Yeah, an' those burner men couldn't a moved faster if I put a blowtorch to their asses."

Chips turned to Winthrop.

"I think we got some extra revs on the screw on time for ya. Can't tell for sure."

Disoriented, Winthrop pulled his thoughts to the present. "Thanks for the help," Winthrop said. "It was a long shot, but all I could think of." His face pinched with concern.

To his relief, Chips changed the conversation's focus.

"Least ya didn't blow the whistle like Randolph did once. That woulda scared half the crew. It was so early in the mornin'."

"That happened with the hospital ship," Randolph said. "Heh, heh. The old man was on the bridge in a microsecond. Of course it was daytime and the crew was awake."

The table started talking about past ship handling incidents and collisions at sea. Winthrop drifted off, his own incident spinning in his head along with images of Mary. He fiddled with his food.

~

Captain Ridgeway said nothing to Winthrop about the event. Certainly he heard of the near-collision. At his first encounter with the old man the morning after the event, Captain Ridgeway looked at him a bit funny. That was it.

Or was Winthrop's head playing tricks on him?

Perhaps the incident prompted a correction and the brass did not make an issue of his erroneous maneuver because they knew they had created the situation. Winthrop gave himself various excuses not to go up to the old man's sea cabin, knock on the door, and discuss the incident.

It was too late. What if the captain didn't know about it? Why open that can of worms, Winthrop?

More than his close call with *Sanctuary,* this event, absurd in its improbability, the stuff of nightmares, would stay with him for life. Always he would wonder could he have handled the scenario better. His rational mind advised him no, but the agony of the near collision stayed, and the doubt remained with it.

~

On June 24, *Eldorado* steamed away from the combat zone, once more destined for Subic Bay. With the *Kitty Hawk* trouble behind him, *Winthrop* relished seeing Mary. *He could talk to her about the near disaster. She would listen, sooth his self-reproach.*

Winthrop expected his remaining stint in the Navy to be tame. After visiting Mary, he could luxuriate in the long transit home to San Diego. The war was over for him. He looked forward to spending his remaining months of active duty in San Diego and the local waters, helping to train a new crew and bringing his part of the vessel to ship shape condition for the next trip to WESTPAC. When *Eldorado* headed out to Vietnam next time, he would be driving back home, a civilian.

It wasn't to be. Destiny and his country required service in the combat zone one more time.

28

At officers call that morning the XO announced the relief ship, *Mount McKinley,* had a breakdown, needed repairs, and wouldn't arrive to relieve *Eldorado* until the end of July. Winthrop's future held more war-zone steaming.

Despite the stultifying tropical heat filling the air as the flagship tied up to the pier at Subic Naval Base, Winthrop's spirits rose. He looked forward to seeing Mary. After sea-and-anchor detail he hurried to the quarter deck. He stood close by as the base civilian workers installed the one telephone line provided for the crew's use.

He grabbed the device when they finished, glanced at the in-port OOD who grinned, and dialed Mary's residence.

"Litton residence," Sue-sue the maid answered.

"Hi, it's Fred Winthrop. Is Mary there?"

"Oh my," she said. "Just a minute."

Mrs. Litton came on the line.

"Fred, Fred, is that you? You didn't get her letter? She's gone back to college."

Mrs. Litton explained that her daughter's roommates wrote and told her they had a cool apartment off campus and to come and enjoy the rest of the summer before classes.

"Mary's excited about seeing you when you get to the States," she said.

"We've been extended here for another month," Winthrop said. "Well, thank you Mrs. Litton."

A deflated Winthrop hung up.

Flagship

Does absence make the heart grow fonder or does privation create the qualms of commitment?

The crew's lagging mail caught up with the ship in the afternoon. Winthrop received Mary's letter. Her message stayed upbeat. She hoped he would visit her when *Eldorado* returned to the States the first part of July. They could spend a lot of time together, before her classes began, she wrote.

In his response he told her of his wish to at least get to her campus by the end of August. An uneasy Winthrop wondered if he could get annual leave and reach Ohio before September.

Winthrop didn't know what to think. Her letter encouraged him to visit her in Oxford, Ohio, home of her campus for Miami University of Ohio. He accumulated some leave which he planned to use when *Eldorado* got back to the States. He wanted to visit her, but now with the delay, she might be back in class by the time he flew home to Syracuse, retrieved his car and drove out to Ohio on his way back to San Diego.

Although he wrote to her about the postponement of the relief, would her return letter reach him before *Eldorado* left for the States? With *Eldorado's* arrival in the States months away, how could he communicate with her. How far can such a brief affair as theirs carry them? He felt her slipping away.

Winthrop spent the off-work hours with Jay Dunston and Steve Van Valkenburg, his stateroom mate, at the O club. None were married but Van Valkenburg had a fiancée back home and Dunston's girlfriend kept him encouraged with her letters. Winthrop brooded about Mary.

Dunston with his similar concerns listened with some understanding.

"I guess if I still care for her, I can't do any whoring, horny as I am, but the whole thing is a long shot. Suppose she meets some college kid. She's young and as hot-blooded as I am."

Dunston nodded. "Got the same problem. Cindy's spicy letters cooled off recently, not as explicit. They're still warm though, so I hope she stays away from dating other guys. Can only hope."

The call of duty Winthrop reflected, involved a profound commitment. The glamor of naval service attracted him and his draft obligation required him to sign up. Only now did he realize the possible cost to him. The *Kitty Hawk* thing scared the hell out of him. He judged the earlier incident with *Sanctuary* as the other ship's fault. The circumstances leading up to his decision to turn to port right into the jaws of collision with the carrier and the oiler seemed instead an act of God.

I'm not immortal.

Death for him could be closer than he once thought. The unpredictable happened in this world. Poor mortals like him remained subject to the whims of destiny.

He recalled a young officer, transferred off *Kitty Hawk* for the Navy's convenience, who joined his wardroom group for the transit back to Subic. The ex-pilot told the guys at Winthrop's table he gave up his wings as an F-4 pilot after a near crash on the carrier deck. His nerves, he said. He couldn't go on. The Navy would reassign him, he didn't know where yet. World War II shell shock stuff. An individual's limit can be reached anytime and the limit differed among men.

The Marines got it tougher. Hard to turn in your M16 and walk off the battlefield.

Winthrop held the Marines up as a standard for himself. If they could gut-out a deployment, so could he.

No one's shot at me yet.

Mary flew off to college fun leaving Winthrop to endure one more trip to the combat zone before his nebulous plans for the future could go anywhere. Other young men would follow him into the war in Vietnam, others would not. Would their fortunes differ after the war? If they survived, would those who served benefit from their service? Winthrop doubted the existence of any special esteem for veterans. A man's military contribution took shape without any guarantee of laurels.

Duty, Fred. Don't quit now.

~

Seaman Mayer sidetracked Winthrop's worries about his future uncertainties and his relationship with Mary. The ship's legal department notified Winthrop his sailor faced captain's nonjudicial punishment. The captain scheduled mast for the morning of June 29.

Sullivan mouthed off once too often as Mayer returned to the ship one afternoon, so Mayer punched him in the face. The petty officer of the watch on the afterbrow broke up the ensuing melee, called the master at arms, and put them both on report.

Eldorado's dark gray weather decks, her mist gray sides and bulkheads, impeccably maintained, accented by various swaths of brilliant white canvas awnings, white railing trim, white bosun's lace on her quarterdeck, and the flag of the United States flying from her stern, stood out on any pier. Away from home in Subic Bay, the ship created the dignity of an American presence. She was the flagship.

Winthrop pondered the value of the work sailors did to keep her in such shape as head down, he watched his white shoes walk on her deck and ladders leading to the bridge. Nobel and Mayer followed in the solemn procession to captain's mast, not a pleasant experience, but a Navy tradition.

The three reached the port wing of the bridge at 0855 for the 0900 captain's mast. The legal officer, a young JG from the administration department who possessed some legal training, waited holding a file folder. Tom Randolph arrived with Sullivan and his first-class, Hoffman. All wore dress whites.

Captain Ridgeway stepped out from the hatch near his sea cabin, also wearing dress whites. He stood behind a wood podium placed on the deck for the occasion.

"Well," he said, "the charge is fighting, a serious matter."

He addressed Mayer. "Seaman Earnest Mayer, do you have anything to say?"

"No sir. I'm sorry sir."

The captain pivoted. "Mister Winthrop, anything to offer?"

"Mayer is a good sailor sir, works hard, and does his duty."

"And Nobel?" The captain said.

"Mayer is reliable, sir." Nobel said.

"How about you . . . let's see," he took the folder from the legal officer. "Seaman Sean Sullivan, how about you?"

"I'm sorry, sir."

Turning to Randolph he said, "Mister Randolph?"

"Sullivan does what he is ordered to do, sir."

"Nothing else?"

Randolph shook his head.

"Hoffman?"

"Nothing to add, sir."

The legal officer pointed to a document in the folder.

"The chaplain has provided a memo for the record, sir."

The old man read it to himself.

He addressed the two principals. "Do you both realize I can restrict you to the ship for thirty days for this, put you on bread and water for three days, give you a written reprimand, or refer you to special court martial?"

"Yes, sir," they answered in unison.

"Our service under war-time conditions and for long periods has created certain unusual stresses. Under these circumstances the chaplain's recommendation makes sense. I will issue both of you a verbal reprimand."

He addressed the legal officer. "Please change the charge to roughhousing and specify the punishment as a verbal reprimand for each."

Captain Ridgeway then proceeded to chew them out. One might more colorfully describe the process as ripping the two men "new ones."

After the verbal lashing, the old man dismissed Mayer.

He turned to Sullivan. "You're the culprit here. I won't have provoking behavior on my ship. You must realize you are getting a break. Your constant harassment of Seaman Mayer is documented by the chaplain's memo."

The captain commenced another upbraiding more cutting than the first. When he finished Sullivan sported a second "new one."

His final comment to Sullivan: "No print shop for you this time."

~

Nobel

Winthrop snagged Nobel out of the first-class lounge and led him out on the weather deck forward of the boat racks. The officer sat on a

A.J. Converse

hatch cover, pushed up his overseas hat, rubbed his itchy front scalp, and wiped some sweat off his forehead.

"What's this business about Johnson promotin' a fist fight in auto storage?"

He's not too pissed, woulda made me sit. Nobel shuffled his feet. *Should I tell the officer all the details? Maybe spin it a bit.*

"Johnson didn't like Sullivan whispering around about Lee and Mayer having somethin' unnatural going on. Aww, huh." He stuttered. The subject disturbed Nobel.

Don't need to tell him I asked Bode to buddy up.

"Hard to stop those rumors, ya know ruins morale, guys thinkin' two queers is running around the ship."

"Christ," Winthrop said. "That's the last thing we need. Nothing to that, is there?"

"Huh, no. In fact Bode is one of Lee's buddies too. Johnson thought a fight might clear the air."

"I hear Sullivan was raggin' Mayer something about his parents."

"Yeah, that too."

Nobel understood what consternation the discovery of a homosexual aboard ship caused: stress, witch-hunts, and fights, with the men suspecting a queer behind every bulkhead. Homosexuals received prompt separation from the Navy with medical discharges. He figured Winthrop would just as soon keep a lid on the rumors.

"This got anything to do with the print shop opening?" Winthrop said.

"Probably, sir, Sullivan's a hot head. Don't care about anybody but his self."

"I mean did Johnson put the idea in Sullivan's head?"

"Don't think so, sir. Lee wants to strike for the print shop, not Mayer."

Winthrop scratched his head again. "You know when I signed up for OCS, I never thought I'd run into this kind of stuff."

"When you been in for eighteen years, ya realize anything can happen."

"Well the old man reamed Sullivan two new ones, if ya know what I mean, not one, two. We witnessed it. And after mast Mister Randolph told Sullivan if he pulled any crap like that again, he'd be off the ship."

"Yes, sir. Might be the best thing for Mayer too, him poppin' Sully one. He got a lot of respect from his shipmates now. No need for an organized fist fight."

"And Lee's got the print shop." Winthrop frowned, stared at the deck for a minute.

"Yes, sir. We wanted that, right?"

"Humph, tell me if anything else comes up in the ranks about this."

~

Mayer

Bode found him on the forward boat deck chipping paint along the gunnel.

"Here's yer new correspondence course for boatswain's mate third," Bode said.

Mayer stopped working, wiped some sweat off his forehead with his handkerchief, and took the study manual in the other hand.

"Too damn hot for this work," he said. "Gotta get my third-class and order other guys to do it."

207

"Don't study too long after dinner. We gonna hit Olongapo one more time tonight. Lee's comin' too."

"Huh," Mayer said. "Bitch'n, like to get one of them little Filipina chicks in bed. Nothin' like a little leg to make a guy forget captain's mast. The old man chewed me out like a surgeon with a scalpel, slice, dice, chop, dig, scrape, and all."

"You ain't lived till ya been to mast, especially if you gonna be a boatswain's mate. Least he didn't put you on bread and water for three days."

Mayer watched Bode rejoin his work party. *Like to boss other sailors like he does. Better than doin' the chipping and painting.*

He thought of his mother. His mother's letter, received a month after she wrote, when the mail caught up with *Eldorado,* told him of her new group home. In shaky handwriting she thanked him for writing. She reported the Navy Relief Society helped her get the spot. Some anonymous person referred them to her.

The chaplain, he figured.

She sent along a *Wilmington Morning Star* news article. The clip reported Mayer was serving aboard the amphibious flagship *Eldorado* in the South China Sea. A shiver ran through him each time he thought of what she wrote: *Your father would have been proud.*

He had posted his answer the day before. He told her of his sentry duty in out-of-the-way places, his friends on the ship, and a little about the Bangkok sights, not about the girls.

Mayer considered himself a regular part of the crew now. *Think I've found a home.*

He went back to chipping.

~

Johnson

Pleased with his maneuvers to help Lee, boatswain's mate second-class Jerome, no middle name, Johnson, stood, hands behind his back, fingering his razor. *Ya did alright, Slim, ya did alright. 'Course Nobel and Winthrop helped with their recommendations, but ya got Sullivan out of the runnin'.*

Johnson thought of his kids, and Leticia. She forced him to join the Navy, the second best decision of his life.

A career, someday I be getting' me one o' those chief's hats.

Don't need this straight edge razor no more.

He decided to keep the lethal weapon for a while longer.

I'll dump it at sea on our way back to the States.

~

At breakfast the following day Winthrop and Randolph discussed the mast.

"Wish I took notes," Winthrop said. "The old man is a virtuoso ass chewer."

Randolph laughed. "A great call, straightened out Sully. And blocking his bid for the print shop stunned Sully the most. I added something when we came down from mast."

"I heard," Winthrop said.

"I told him one more incident like that and I would personally see he got kicked off the ship."

"Mister Larsen," Chips said, "ya might take note of that."

"I did, I did. Learn something new each day, Chipper." Larsen folded his skinny arms and leaned back in his chair.

~

After breakfast, before the announcement for sea and anchor detail, Winthrop checked the deck office. He found a message in his basket from the captain's office, the personnel part of the ship's administration division. The note verified Seaman Zackery Lee's transfer to the print shop when *Eldorado's* relief ship arrived.

He stopped by admin, down the passage from the deck department. Crammed with personnel files and men on typewriters, the place wielded some power. Winthrop made sure to chat with the sailor who handled his file. Retaining the man's goodwill helped a lot toward keeping his own personnel record accurate. Not that the personnel guys would ever mess up one's file, Winthrop figured a rapport with the guy generated more attention to his record than average.

He picked up some information too. Another yeoman in the office told him the executive officer dropped the requirement for the print shop to supply a man to work on the mess deck.

"Reilly told me he needs the time for on-the-job training," the man said. "His third-class, Odell, has orders to the staff at Subic Bay. Reilly wants Lee working right away. Anyway the admiral's chief of staff put in a word to the XO. You know Reilly. He probably BS'd the guy."

~

At 0900, *Eldorado* threw off all lines and departed Subic Bay, setting a course for Vietnam. Winthrop's nerves settled down after a few watches. Ennui filled him instead. He found some relief in activity. He plugged along with the daily routine, doing extra stuff to keep busy.

After breakfast on the second day out of port, Winthrop went by the chaplain's office. He entered through a small compartment functioning as the ship's library in officers' country. He tapped on the open door.

Lieutenant Commander Stanley Koehler, chaplain corps, looked up from his desk and stopped writing. He stared over his spectacles, frumpled hair covering a balding head.

"Yes, Mister Winthrop."

"Aww, sir, don't know what you wrote, but thank you for helping Mayer. He needed a break."

Koehler shrugged. "Part of my job."

Winthrop glanced at some *Playboy* magazines stacked in the corner. "*Playboy,*" he said, raising an eyebrow.

"I get it for the articles."

"I see."

"How's your man Johnson doing?"

"Okay, why'd you ask?"

"Oh nothing," the chaplain said. "Understand your girl went back to college," he added.

"Huh, yes sir."

"We all face these challenges. Makes us stronger. You're a good man, Mister Winthrop. Things will work out."

Maybe there is more to this guy than I thought.

Winthrop, in a better mood, walked out of the chaplain's office.

211

29

Operation Beacon Torch which ended July 2 cost the Marines from special landing force Alpha 13 killed in action and 123 wounded. The brass claimed 86 enemy kills and the capture of 40 tons of rice stores. It troubled Winthrop that the Marines, as they retracted, spotted communist army units reoccupying the same area cleared by the attack. The whole deal turned out to be a pointless exercise for the special landing force.

The Bear Bite operation didn't impress Winthrop either. The assault produced only minor successes. The initial landing and its three follow-on maneuvers yielded 18 communists killed and 59 prisoners taken. By the time special landing force Bravo retracted they had lost 3 Marines and suffered a total of 51 casualties.

The troops killed bad guys and took some prisoners, but failed to clear the territory for good.

Winthrop reflected on the disdain that allowed the brass to sacrifice Marines like so much ordnance for such paltry results. These were American lives that could never be replaced, not bombs which can be manufactured cheaply by a factory somewhere.

~

The grunts got no respite. At 1030 July 3 Winthrop hustled to his battle station on *Eldorado's* bridge as the Alpha force deployed for the start of operation Bear Claw. They landed in eastern Quang Tri Province, which abutted up to the demilitarized zone. The Bravo force landed nearby the next day to start operation Beaver Track. Winthrop witnessed America and the communist North mixed it up again and again with no quarter given.

212

Flagship

On the fourth of July in the Far East, a day before American people would eat hot dogs and barbeque at home, Winthrop and his shipmates steamed close to the Vietnamese coast near the DMZ, eleven time zones away, headed for anchorage in Da Nang. The ship anchored at 0645.

Winthrop, standing the morning watch, spotted a pattern of liquid, like a light sprinkling of rain appear on the decks as if an illusion. Unlike rain droplets, the substance spread thin, not beading, and lay on the deck in the sun for a moment. In the next instant the stuff vanished, evaporated on the hot decks. Winthrop wondered if it fell at all. No clouds floated in the tropical morning sky. It was blue and clear.

Solvent of some sort?

Sailors on the forward boat deck showed a brief interest before continuing their work when it disappeared.

~

After the watch Winthrop ate lunch in the wardroom, not certain he had seen anything at all. He mentioned the possible mirage to his table mates.

"Overspray," Merlin Chandler said. "They've been spraying that Agent Orange junk all around. Maybe some carried in the breeze over us. No sweat, the stuff kills plants but not humans."

"Supposed to reduce the cover for the commies," Chips said. "They're spraying all over the place."

"Futile, I guess," Winthrop said, "Like all the other stuff we're doing."

Chandler took a second serving of *giniling* from Ocampo and said, "Cheer up. We'll be headed home soon."

~

At 1900 on July 6 Eldorado weighed anchor once more and set a course for the amphibious objective area near the DMZ. The flagship arrived that evening and commenced her back and forth runs in a holding pattern just off the coast. Winthrop and his shipmates continued the monotonous work for hours in the humid conditions. By then the salt rings under his arms had become permanent stains on his wash khakis. The ship's laundry had given up any effort to remove them. He lit cigarette after cigarette promising himself he would quit when he got back to the States. The day, Wednesday, could have been any day. It merged with yesterday and tomorrow.

~

Mayer

After breakfast on July 7, Mayer and Bode sat at a table on the mess deck with a second cup of coffee.

"I can get you off sentry duty," Bode said. "Winthrop and Randolph should agree to put Sullivan on sentry replacing you. He needs to learn that mast is not the only consequence to spreading rumors and bad mouthin' a shipmate."

"Ya think?" Mayer said.

"I think they'll put you back on lookout when we're at anchor. Least you don't have to shoulder that damn M-1. Those antiques are heavy."

"It's okay. Anyway I wrote my mom. Told her I was standin' sentry duty. And I still stand lookout underway."

Mayer figured he best stay with a low profile for a while, to keep out of trouble.

Bode shrugged. "Suit yourself. So how are ya doin' on the correspondence course?"

214

"Good, I think I can pass the third-class test."

"Gotta check on my work party." Bode said and left Mayer thinking about making third-class and reenlisting.

~

Johnson

Johnson surveyed the mess compartment. Steel tables bolted to the deck with attached steel chairs, not luxurious but comfortable enough. Except for periods of intense dangerous work, the seagoing life appealed to him. The ship provided good chow and restful racks. The berthing areas were crowded, but got better with each promotion. His kids could respect his career. Not many good careers for guys like him from the Detroit projects.

He wanted to take the first-class exam. In a month he would have completed three years as a second-class. He could take the exam if he got the recommendation. The process went up the chain of command. He figured Nobel would back him and thus Winthrop. Clear sailing from there, Lieutenant Trucker would recommend him. So the captain would approve it. Would Commander Webber intervene? He heard the XO wanted him off the ship after that 1 MC announcement on the way to Subic. He needed the man on his side. *Another white guy.*

Nobel stopped by his table, took a seat.

"Ya know Winthrop asked me about the fist fight you were promotin'," he said.

"How'd he find out?"

"It was all over the mess decks man. You know sailors. You better learn that, ya wanna be a first-class."

"That gets to the XO, my promotion's dead."

"That's why ya need friends in this here Navy. I think I muddied up Winthrop's reasoning enough so's he'll drop it."

"Thanks man."

"So how's the wife and kids?" Nobel said.

~

Nobel

He had him now. Johnson's a buddy, Nobel thought as he walked to the first-class lounge. More than that, he knew Johnson believed he owed Nobel.

He spotted Hoffman in the first-class lounge, walked over and sat next to him.

"This deployment shit's gettin' old," Nobel said.

"Yeah," Hoffman said. "We shoulda been on the way back to the States by now."

"Least we ain't Marines. Westmoreland's usin' 'em up."

"Of course, he's Army ain't he?"

Nobel stretched, rubbed an old scar on his chin.

"Yeah, and he's blinded by his own BS. He's got the president's backing though."

"President don't know nothin'. He's a politician. If he was smart, he'd turn the whole thing over to the Air Force. Bomb the shit outta 'em."

Noble laughed. "What would you an' I do if they ended it that fast?"

"Aw, crap, Nobel, there'll always be a Navy."

30

Operation Bear Claw and its follow-on operations with other Marine units from the I Corps area ended on July 14. The maneuvers and attacks produced 424 North Vietnamese kills and cost the alpha SLF 8 dead and 179 wounded Marines. SLF bravo Marines lost 16 men in Beaver Track but killed 176 of the North Vietnamese Army. *Eldorado* had spent the time moving between the active operational area and Da Nang, anchoring briefly at the key base on July 9 and July 11.

Things never seem to go as planned and Winthrop got involved in a SNAFU. On July 9 at 1300, the admiral ordered *Eldorado*, having anchored a few hours earlier at 0800, underway. A problem arose. Some of the amphibious group commander's staff members were ashore, supposedly on business. They had taken an early morning boat ride to the pier.

The boatswain's mate of the watch came on the 1MC, blew his pipe and announced, "Lieutenant junior grade Winthrop to the bridge, Lieutenant junior grade Winthrop to the bridge."

Winthrop, finishing his lunch after the morning watch, heard the broadcast.

What now? Am I gonna hear about the Kitty Hawk *incident?*

He hustled out to the weather deck, climbed two levels of ladders and arrived puffing, on the port wing. Captain Ridgeway, agitation on his face, shuffled around near the pelorus. He motioned Winthrop over to where he stood.

"Aw, Fred, some of the staff officers are over in Da Nang. They're supposed to be back by now. Think they're at the club. We have to get underway now. Go find them and get them back here."

"Aye, sir, I'll get the OMB crew."

"Take my gig. The crew's waiting down here. He pointed to the accommodation ladder on the quarterdeck. Stay in touch on the radio. I'm calling out the sea and anchor detail. We'll weigh anchor soon as you get back."

Winthrop hustled down to the quarterdeck and down the accommodation ladder, and boarded the gig saying, "Let's go," to the coxswain.

The pier was a mile away to the south.

"Head south."

He planned to find his way to the O club once he landed, track them down, and haul them back regardless of rank, a job he relished.

The gig, modern, slick, fast, raced away toward the pier.

Three quarters of the way, Winthrop spotted a spiffy looking craft, probably the staff gig returning with the missing officers. He ordered his boat to slow and picked up a battery powered bull horn stowed nearby.

"Ahoy the boat, ahoy the boat," he blasted on the bull horn.

The other boat slowed. As it got closer, Winthrop spotted the group. All but the boat crew were officers.

"Who are you?" Winthrop challenged on the bull horn.

An officer he recognized, wearing a hat with the gold scrambled eggs of a commander, shouted in a drunken voice, "Who the fuck wants to know?"

Winthrop responded, "Mister Winthrop, sir, from *Eldorado*. I have orders to find you. *Eldorado* is getting underway."

The commander, somewhat chastised, answered. "Very well."

Winthrop picked up his radio handset.

"*Eldorado,* this is Eldorado One, over."

His ship didn't respond. *Some screw-up with the radio.*

In the blind Winthrop announced, *"Eldorado*, this is Eldorado One. The staff gig is returning to the ship. I am returning also."

The message must have been received. The anchor cleared the water as the staff gig, running ahead of him, landed at the accommodation ladder. By the time Winthrop landed, the staff boat was being hoisted to the forward boat deck. His own crew took the gig forward, to be next in line for the boom. Minutes later, *Eldorado* steamed out of the harbor back toward the demilitarized zone.

Winthrop climbed up to the bridge to his station for the sea and anchor detail. He never learned what happened to the wandering staff, but judging from Captain Ridgway's countenance when Winthrop arrived on the bridge, the plastered officers were in deep trouble.

"Thank you, Fred, go ahead and take the conn. I believe I'll sit out here for a time."

With that the old man mounted his pedestal chair on the port wing and put his feet up on the rail.

~

Nobel

Nobel stood forward under the five-inch gun mount with the anchor gang and watched as the two boats returned to *Eldorado*.

"Stand-by on the boom," he shouted to the boom winch operator.

Nearby, the windlass, a powerful wench device used to haul in the anchor, stood ready.

"Stand-by on the anchor windlass," Nobel told the operator. Then, "Test the anchor windlass."

The crew turned on the power with the wildcat disengaged. Next the anchor gang released the first safety stopper and tested the wildcat itself, a device which encircled the windlass with built in cavities, each designed to hold a link and thus grip the chain as the windlass turned. The gang then released the other stopper, leaving the windlass and its wildcat alone to hold the chain fast.

"Ready to heave in," Noble reported to the bridge via the talker.

The order came, "Heave around."

Nobel motioned to the assigned sailor who turned on the powerful windlass. It started pulling the anchor chain onto the ship, delivering it in a continuous stream to the chain locker below decks. The men stood back. If the chain ever snapped, any of the thirty-five-pound links could kill a man. Nobel knew the chain had been strength tested the last time the ship was in the States, but the ship's many anchoring operations had put it through unusual strain.

A sudden, brief slack announced the anchor had broken free from the bottom.

Nobel turned to the talker. "Anchor's aweigh."

The talker repeated it to the bridge.

As the anchor neared the hawse two sailors sprayed it with a fire hose to clean off the mud.

Via the talker Nobel reported, "Anchor housed."

By then the staff gig crew had aligned it under the boom, tied to the sea painter line which ran from the ship to the gig's bow. The crew attached the hoist cables. For safety, each grabbed a knotted rope known as a monkey line strung from a cross piece on the hoist cables. The boat coxswain gave Nobel a wave.

Nobel raised his right hand, giving the boom winch operator the signal to hoist the boat.

As the staff gig cleared the rail above, the crew of the captain's gig positioned their vessel below. A deck sailor tossed the sea painter down to the bow man who made it fast.

Nobel motioned the sailors near the quarterdeck to hoist the accommodation ladder and secure it to the gunnel.

~

Mayer

Mayer watched as the boom positioned the staff boat and the gig crew dropped their monkey lines. One tossed him a rope. He used it to guide the craft to its skids next to the admiral's barge. The craft settled snug on its spot and the crew hopped down to help secure it for sea. The physical and hazardous work on the deck force invigorated Mayer.

His stomach growled in anticipation of lunch on the mess decks. *Ya work hard, but ya eat well.*

~

Johnson

Johnson watched as the admiral paced around his private veranda deck forward of and below the bridge, a frown on his face. When the two gigs approached, he turned and stalked to his quarters inside.

On the bridge, Johnson bounced up and down on his tired feet, stimulating them, trying to work out the dull pain rising up from the steel deck. He no longer did the manual work of the deck force, but the long hours of standing for his watches wore him down. Yet he felt some pride

221

for his ship and the first division sailors, enough, anyway he thought, to keep him going.

Of course, there's the chow and I don't have to cook it and clean up after. Mess cooks do that.

He glanced over at Winthrop who had arrived minutes before and stood nearby, his attention on the captain's gig, now being hoisted aboard.

Not a bad officer, I guess. I've had worse.

~

After the brief anchorage at Da Nang on July 11 the flagship returned to the amphibious objective area to get the admiral close to the action and to keep *Eldorado* on the move for security reasons.

On Saturday July 15 following protocol, *Eldorado* returned and anchored in Da Nang harbor in the early morning. She didn't stay long.

Winthrop, at lunch, stopped, his fork half-way to his mouth, as the announcement came over the 1MC, "Now station the sea and anchor detail. Make preparations to get under way."

"Christ, we just anchored," he said.

"Duty calls," Larsen said.

Winthrop wolfed down a couple of bites, took a swig of milk, and stood as he wiped his chin and tossed the napkin on the table. Larsen, already on his way, stopped and waited for him.

The old man met them on the bridge.

"The NVA attacked the airfield this morning with rockets," he said. "We can't risk the flagship. Those damn rockets can reach us."

By 1300 *Eldorado* steamed out of the harbor. A later secret message on the OOD board clarified the extent of the surprise attack. Eight American's were killed, 175 wounded, ten aircraft destroyed, and 49 damaged. The report identified the rockets as Soviet built 120mm and 140mm and fired by VC units from north of the base parameter. The North Vietnamese army and its VC irregulars operated with impunity in the jungles around the base.

Like cockroaches, if you saw one VC, you knew hundreds or even thousands more scurried around the area. President Johnson's failing main strategy, the escalation thing, exhibited a major flaw in and around Da Nang. The idea of piling more and more US servicemen into the country to overwhelm the enemy only created more targets and North Vietnam generated an endless supply of cockroaches.

The president's sporadic bombing of the North inspired the anti-war and other fifth-column elements subverting the war effort at home. A terrible thing, Winthrop thought, to have your own countrymen resisting the war effort, in effect working for the enemy, and to have an incompetent president flailing and dithering at the same time.

The escalation seemed to be all on the North's side. Their attacks in South Vietnam became more frequent and more deadly. Still Johnson refused to take the war to the enemy's homeland in sufficient ferocity.

~

The brass weren't beaten. They wielded the amphibious ready group again and again to launch Marines at the enemy. The flagship sounded general quarters and manned battle stations at 0530 July 20. Special landing force Bravo landed near Quang Tri City, targeting the area between it and the city of Hue. Mission: destroy the Viet Cong 806th battalion. The assault, called Bear Chain, pushed the VC into an ambush by the army of the Republic of Vietnam.

223

The Vietnamese allies mauled the VC battalion which left 252 of their own dead on the battlefield. The cost to America, light in military parlance, but troubling to Winthrop, numbered nine brave Marines and two Navy corpsmen. The message which Winthrop read on the bridge did not mention the South Vietnamese army. Winthrop figured the allies suffered substantial casualties.

Special landing force Alpha followed Bravo and landed July 21 on a search and destroy mission in the same area. The inscrutable military naming protocol called the attack Beacon Guide. The Marines took no losses and encountered no enemy. On July 24, while Marines and Navy corpsmen slogged through jungles and rice paddies pursuing an elusive enemy *Eldorado* left the area. She anchored for replenishment in Da Nang at 0800 on July 25.

The captain ordered flight quarters once the ship anchored. Second division organized a congo line and *Eldorado* received supplies by air. A chopper hovered above the flight deck and lowered provisions in a cargo net. The hearty men in the line stretching down to the stores compartment unloaded and deposited dozens of boxes filled with food. With the supplies aboard, the captain called out the sea-and-anchor detail. At 1130 the flagship weighed anchor and proceeded back to the amphibious objective area.

Once outside the harbor, Captain Ridgway turned the conn over to Winthrop and retired to his cabin. Tom Randolph relieved Winthrop at noon. *Eldorado* joined the other amphibious ready group ships in the operational area later in the day.

As Winthrop's sea legs acclimated to the steady light yaw of coastal steaming once again he began to doubt the existence of a relief ship.

Flagship

Would the Mount Mac really show up?

The next day, July 26, the exhausted Marines of SLF Bravo returned to sea and boarded the ready group ships without having engaged the enemy.

A good omen? Winthrop hoped so.

For the flagship and her worn-out crew, service in the combat zone neared completion. Light appeared at the end of the tunnel. Round-eyed women, homecoming bands, flag waving, and mom's apple pie beckoned in even the toughest sailor's dreams. *Eldorado* steamed toward Da Nang one last time for a rendezvous with her relief, the USS *Mount McKinley*.

31

On July 27, at 0630 *Eldorado* anchored in Da Nang harbor, expecting the USS *Mount McKinley* to arrive from Subic Bay within twenty-four hours. Once the flag transferred over, *Eldorado* would head for the Philippines port for fuel and supplies, then home to the States.

That night in the darkness of the bridge Winthrop eyed the quartermaster as he bent over the chart under a dim red light, marking bearings, checking for drifting or dragging. *Eldorado* lay silent, tugging on its anchor in Da Nang harbor, the regular sentries posted, waterline lights rigged, and an anti-swimmer picket boat patrolling.

A trickle of perspiration rolled down his back giving him a reminder of the tropical conditions. He wiped sweat off his brow, pulled off his piss-cutter and examined the growing wet mark and salt stains along the edge. Bored, tired, a strange dread in the atmosphere he sensed around him, the recent rocket attacks at the airfield preying on his mind, he understood his duty. If rockets started falling on his ship he would sound general quarters. One thing about a ship, no foxholes existed for cover. The three-quarter-inch steel making up *Eldorado*'s hull provided scant protection compared to six feet of earth.

Winthrop replaced his hat and surveyed the men on the bridge, sleepy, inattentive.

How fast could they react?

Johnson, his boatswain's mate, lounged against the magnetic compass pedestal, awake, barely alert.

"Johnson," he said, "how about checking on the lookouts?"

"Aye, aye, sir," Johnson said, pulling himself off the pedestal. "Getting bored standing around. Tomorrow, eh Mister Winthrop," he said and grinned.

"Tomorrow, indeed, shipmate," Winthrop answered and went back to his thoughts.

So I sound GQ, then what?

The old man would take over. Winthrop wondered about the picket boat. Would the captain want to get the men aboard or order them to head for the shoreline? A damn rocket attack could come out of the sky without warning.

Order them to the beach.

Winthrop figured he should, before the old man got to the bridge.

~

Something wrong now.

The thought hit him out of nowhere. Despite the hot tropical night a chill wave washed over the young watch officer.

We're going home soon. Why tonight? Just my mind playing tricks on me.

He forced his thoughts to jump to the transit over to San Diego. The Sundays would be real days for holiday routine, with cookouts on the after-boat deck. Nothing like a steak cooked in a half oil drum, jury rigged into a grill, Navy beans, potato salad, all the stuff. No beer, but what the hell. And cool weather out on the Pacific Ocean, cool weather.

Where the hell is the picket boat?

He had heard the steady churn of "*Eldorado* one," its radio call sign, every ten minutes as the boat with its armed crew circled the flagship on a unhurried track, the sound comforting in its way. The port running light glowed red as the craft had circled counter-clockwise around the flagship. Now silence and darkness surrounded him.

The question hammered Winthrop. *Where's the picket boat?* The terror of battle loomed somewhere out in the tropical night. When his last leave ended and he said his good-byes to his folks, his old man said, "The sea will challenge you, but you possess enough guts to succeed, Fred. And you'll survive aboard ship. The grunts on the beach are the ones dying in Vietnam."

"The grunts are the ones dying," his father said.

The tentacles of this crazy war drew America's best young men into jungle death. Nearing the end of his tour, Winthrop's physical self remained unscathed by the meat-grinder war. Ship handling provided challenges enough, even death defying tests of his judgement. Prickles of stinging sweat dripped over the chilling goose bumps running up his back.

Where's the picket boat? Is this it? Is this the night I die?

Winthrop's every sense awake, alert, he took a breath. He strained to hear. He strained to see something of the anti-swimmer picket boat circling *Eldorado* in the night.

Should see its running lights, crap.

Only an instant had passed since the first realization hit him.

Something is wrong, bad. Where's that boat?

Swimmers, the highest threat, or small craft, blackened inflatable boats, and underwater rebreathers all threatened. Damn, what's going on?

He forgot about the rockets. He moved toward the 21MC. *Check with combat.*

Winthrop flipped the lever for CIC. "Combat, conn, how about a radio check with the picket boat."

"Combat, aye."

Winthrop walked over to Harley Larsen.

"Standby man, somethin's goin' on," he said.

Larsen nodded. "Where's Johnson?"

"Out checking the lookouts."

"Maybe I ought to check the sentries."

"Not yet, standby, somethings up."

The 21MC squawked. "Conn, combat, the picket boat doesn't answer."

Winthrop left Larsen standing in the wheelhouse and went out on the starboard wing. With his binoculars he scanned the sea in the semidarkness lit only by a waning moon. He trotted over to the port wing and did the same.

"Call up the sentries," he said to the bridge talker. "Can they spot the picket boat?"

"Aye, sir."

After a minute the talker reported. "No sign of the picket boat, sir."

His fear materialized. The talker shouted, "Port quarter sentry reports men coming over the side!"

All the preparation for deployment the year before, all the hazards and demands of the previous months seemed but zephyrs. This real attack pressed Winthrop past fatigue, past concern, past fear toward instinct alone. The enemy assault materialized in the night as boarders climbing the sides near the stern where the deck came closest to the water. *VC probably.*

Where's the fucking picket boat?

Winthrop turned to Larsen. "Sound general quarters. Tell 'em boarders port quarter!"

Winthrop raced to the port wheelhouse hatch, leaped through and headed aft pulling his Ithaca .45 as he ran.

Larsen hit the switch and the loud, steady bongs started. "Bong, bong, bong . . ." A shaky voice sang throughout the ship on the 1 MC: "Repel boarders, repel boarders! Boarders on the port quarter, boarders on the port quarter! General quarters, general quarters, all hands man your battle stations."

Eldorado practiced to repel boarders during her operational readiness inspection before deploying to WESTPAC. The drills, almost an afterthought in training, harkened back to tactics in the days of wooden sailing ships.

Winthrop prayed the men could handle this attack. The armory would open, but who would grab a gun and rush to the stern? Training demanded the men head for their assigned battle stations. He doubted the assignments to the repel borders team were up to date. Not only had the senior watch officer retired but the crew, too busy fighting the war, hadn't drilled to repel boarders in months. Winthrop hoped his automatic pistol and Mayer's M1 could hold the attackers at the port quarter until other armed sailors arrived.

He wielded the gun wildly, feeling for the safety with his thumb, and flicking it off as his ran. Flashes appeared near the stern. Silhouetted shapes appeared on the gunnel. He fired off a shot in that direction, reached the ladder to the deck above Mayer on the run, and like a deck sailor, slid down its edges, holding his .45 against one rail and his free hand on the other. He hit the deck, and sprinted to close the short distance to the next ladder.

230

Flagship

~

The nexus of two points of time nearly 25 years and a half a world apart merged at that instant in a minute lump of a weld, painted deck gray and barely noticeable in the dark. Lieutenant junior grade Fredrick Winthrop, an ordinary college-boy reserve Naval officer, two years out of college, racing to protect his ship, stumbled on an irregular weld, ugly, but "good enough for government work," created by an otherwise meticulous wielder in a North Carolina shipyard in 1943. The welder, John Mayer happened to be the missing-in-action father of Seaman Earnest Mayer, port quarter sentry.

Stumbling, flailing, Winthrop continued, desperate now, as he reached the ladder leading to Mayer's level. Arms thrashing, Winthrop managed to fire another shot from his automatic as he clambered down toward Mayer's position. The sailor's dark shape appeared behind a cowl. Mayer, huddled behind the man-sized vent, brandished his ancient M-1 and peeked out at the attackers as he described the extent of the assault to the bridge talker. Winthrop, in full stride, stumbled into him, shoving him onto the open deck.

Stunned, off balance, Mayer pointed his weapon at the attackers and managed a shot before falling with a VC bullet in his brain. Winthrop fired once from behind the cowl vent, squatted, and tried to drag Mayer to safety. Shots came from his left, as the starboard quarter sentry fired at the VC sappers.

Dressed in loincloth, covered with black grease, the boarders fired back. A shape moved from the stern and grabbed a sapper. The man disappeared in the darkness. Lights appeared, battle lanterns, then the roar of a heavy weapon sounded immediately above Winthrop. He turned and looked up toward the shooter. Boatswain mate first-class

231

Nobel stood at the top of the ladder barefoot, wearing only skivvies and firing a Browning automatic rifle. The blur of action surrounded Winthrop. He remained squatting, frozen, next to the lifeless Mayer.

Captain Ridgway showed up in slippers, T-shirt, and work khaki pants. He shouted orders to the men with battle lanterns to shine them on the bloody scene.

"Mister Winthrop," he commanded, "Get to the bridge. Call out the doctor and corpsmen to the stern."

With a quick "Aye, sir," Winthrop raced back to the bridge.

He grabbed the bridge microphone saying to Larsen, "Think we stopped them," and spoke to the MIC, "Ship's doctor and all corpsmen to the stern, ships doctor and all corpsmen to the stern."

Minutes rushed by. Winthrop stood gripping the MIC. Ensign Larsen took charge of responding to "manned and ready" reports from the crew.

We stopped 'em.

The rest blurred in Winthrop's mind. Moments could have been hours before Captain Ridgeway appeared and took the microphone.

"This is the captain speaking. We have successfully defended the ship from a direct attack, my personal commendation to all of you for your quick response. We lost a crewman in the action, Seaman Earnest Mayer of the first division. In a moment we will secure from general quarters. Keep him and his family in your prayers tonight."

At some point, Johnson returned to the bridge. Inasmuch as a black man could be pale, Johnson was pale.

The picket boat came alongside after the shooting with a grease-covered Vietcong sapper in custody. The boat had left its assigned route around the ship to save an apparent drowning fisherman who turned out to be a planned distraction for the enemy attack. The captain ordered the prisoner held in the ship's brig. The picket boat returned to its patrol duty.

At 0400, LTJG Tom Reynolds assumed the watch on the bridge. Winthrop went below and hit the sack.

32

Reveille woke Winthrop at 0600. Sleepy, he walked down the passage to the officer's head and showered. Back in his stateroom he dressed in fresh khakis, put on his shoes, the routine he had followed countless times, and realized that the events of the night before were like nothing he would ever again witness nor forget.

Out of order rumbling thoughts and images of the attack flashed around his head. The visual of Mayer's lifeless eyes staring as Winthrop dragged him to the cover of the air vent dissolved to the sound of the bridge talker: "Port quarter sentry reports men coming over the side!"

As Winthrop arrived in the wardroom, a few steps from his stateroom, officers stood around, not sitting, just standing and talking in groups which formed and dissolved as members sought coffee refills from pots warming on the mess counter. None sat at the tables in the customary manner. Energy, pulsating like in an electric grid, filled the place. The stewards hustled around setting the tables for breakfast talking among themselves, sometimes in Tagalog, sometimes in English. A small circle of animated officers huddled with Harley Larsen, turned to greet Winthrop as he entered.

The XO arrived and asked everyone to be seated. He stood until everyone reached their tables. Instead of sitting first like wardroom etiquette required, he asked the rest to sit as he remained standing.

"The captain asked me to update you on last night's attack," he said. "Apparently a six-man team of VC sappers attempted to disable *Eldorado* either by placing a satchel charge on the aircraft fueling tanks under the flight deck or by getting the charge into after-steering where it would have destroyed our steering gears.

"Our picket boat captured one of the attackers who pretended to be drowning in order to draw the boat away from the boarding point at the stern. The prisoner is currently in our brig and will be flown today to Da Nang for interrogation by Naval Intelligence.

"The other attackers were killed by the repel boarders crew and our watch-standers. The captain wishes to extend his commendation to those men, including Ensign Larsen and LTJG Winthrop.

"The extra firepower Mister Winthrop brought to the scene helped stop the sappers and Mister Larsen's call to general quarters on the 1MC may now qualify him as a boatswain's mate." A wry smile crossed the commander's face.

The men in the room chuckled with the XO's attempt to lighten the somber moment with a kudo to Larsen's announcement. The absence of BM2 Johnson on the bridge was ignored by all except Winthrop.

With that the XO turned the floor over to the chaplain who said a prayer for Seaman Mayer.

Winthrop ordered his favorite breakfast, poached eggs on toast with grits, hash browns, orange juice and coffee. But he picked at the food, his appetite dulled by the previous night's events, and answered his table mate's questions as well as he could, leaving out the fact that his stumbling caused Mayer's death.

The old warrant officer spoke.

"So, young master Larsen," Chips said, "how was it you called for general quarters?"

Larsen chuckled. "Johnson was out checking the lookouts so Fred dumped the job on me."

The picture of one of the boarders disappearing in the blackness during the attack flared in Winthrop's mind. *Did Johnson get that one?*

Winthrop knew the rumors that Johnson carried a razor hung down his back on a leather thong. *Was he shooting the bull with Lee on the stern when the attack came? A heroic act, taking out a sapper with his razor, but something he wouldn't report. Sailors weren't supposed to carry such personal weapons.*

As Winthrop prepared to leave the wardroom, hoping to hit his rack for a little sleep, the XO approached him.

"Fred," he said, "while its fresh in your mind, the captain would like you to write out a report of the events last night as you remember them. Give it to him first thing this morning."

"Yes, sir. I'll do it right now."

He wrote the report in long hand on some personal stationary at his stateroom desk. He left out the part about seeing an attacker disappear into the blackness, but did report stumbling into Mayer and causing his death.

He finished the report and delivered it to the captain by 0900, and went back to his stateroom to catch some sleep before the 1200 to 0400 watch.

~

The afternoon watch gave Winthrop a chance to reflect on his actions of the night before. An OOD should never leave his watch station until relieved. *Why didn't I follow that rule? But I acted on instinct alone. Where was that in the regulations?*

Had he followed the Navy protocol Mayer might have survived.

The right way, the wrong way, the Navy way, but sometimes you act on instinct. What had Mary told him? Her dad always followed the

Navy way she had said. But then she pointed out her dad had been passed over for admiral.

Ultimately there were no answers. You did the best you could in emergencies. Would the captain agree? Would the old man reprimand him for leaving his post?

Toward the end of the watch Captain Ridgeway stepped out on the bridge and asked Winthrop to stop by his cabin when off duty.

~

"You asked to see me, sir," Winthrop announced after knocking at the captain's open cabin door.

Captain Ridgeway turned from his desk on his swivel chair and motioned for him to sit on the single arm chair in the cramped room.

"Just finishing up my report to the admiral," he said.

Winthrop sat feeling as he had several times in college after a wild party, without anxiety, tired, quiet, and hung over. He waited.

To Winthrop's right was a small table where Ridgeway took his meals. Next to the table the doorway to his private head and shower stood open. On the other side of the old man's desk and nearly flush against it lay his bed. A ship's captain led a Spartan and lonely existence. Yet so many Naval officers aspired for the job.

No speculation entered Winthrop's mind. The man's position, earned after many years of suffering his superior's judgements concerning his performance, demanded only respect.

See what he says.

"Well you left your station," he said. "Might have been better if you stayed on the bridge. But I can't fault you. What made you do it?"

"Can't explain, sir. Instinct, I guess."

The old man held up Winthrop's report, tore it up and tossed it in his trash can.

"My report will become the only official document of the action last night. I've spoken to the others and have a complete picture. When you arrived on the scene Mayer was standing, exposed, with no concern for his own safety, engaging the attackers and protecting his shipmates."

Winthrop shuffled his feet. "I'm terribly sorry sir, about Mayer."

"I'm gonna try to get him a medal, a small consolation for his mother. I'm told she's had a hard time since losing her husband at Normandy."

He looked hard at Winthrop then. "One other thing, Nobel got four of the five sappers with his BAR, quite a feat. But the doc reports one died because his neck was slit."

"Huh, oh."

"We don't issue straight razors to our sailors. You wouldn't know anything about that?"

"No, sir." *Christ, Johnson did get one.*

"Another thing, we're promoting Johnson to first class, he's already taken the test, no reason to delay it. You'll need a new leading petty officer for your division anyway."

"Sir?"

"Noble earned his chief's hat last night, a medal too. How 'bout that, the only one from the old repel borders team to show up. He just grabbed the BAR out of the armory and ran back to the stern, skivvies an' all."

Like all past war stories: The thing about battle is that it is messy. People make mistakes, do the best they can. The official story generally cleans up the reality, creates the legend and that's how people remember it.

Winthrop shook his head, smiled, the sudden insight telling him how the old man made captain.

"That will be all, Mister Winthrop," Ridgeway said. "Thank you for your efforts last night."

33

On July 29, 1967, *Mount McKinley* lay tied up alongside having arrived at 2200 the day before. The admiral's staff transferred the personal effects, files, supplies, and everything portable from *Eldorado* to the relief flagship. Willing crewmembers of *Eldorado* pitched in, upbeat, anticipating a voyage home. Around noon the men heard of a disaster on the USS *Forrestal* which swamped any news going to their hometowns concerning *Eldorado*'s minor skirmish with the Viet Cong two days before.

Forrestal, an attack carrier sending tactical air strikes at North Vietnam from "Yankee Station" where she operated, suffered explosions and fire when an errant Zuni missile fired accidentally from a jet prepping for an air strike. Sketchy details buzzed around the crew. Winthrop read some of the earlier reports on the OOD message board. Over a hundred sailors died in the conflagration either fighting the subsequent fires or in the initial explosions from bombs on the deck. The fire damaged several jets preparing for the strike.

Many read the *Pacific Stars and Stripes* story about the fire when *Eldorado* reached Subic Bay for resupply a few days later. A previously unknown lieutenant commander, one John C. McCain, was mentioned because he was the son of Admiral John S. McCain, currently serving as commander-in-chief, US Naval Forces, Europe. The younger McCain, caught in the cockpit, escaped the fire that engulfed his plane by walking forward on the aircraft's nose and then jumping for his life over the rest of the flames.

Winthrop browsed the final results of operation Beacon Guide, the last amphibious landing overseen by the flagship about the same time as reading the details of the *Forrestal* fire. The VC facing the Bravo landing force had melted away like ghosts. This first unsuccessful attack of the landing force ended July 30, the day after *Eldorado's* admiral transferred his flag to the *Mount Mac*. The Marines suffered no losses.

~

During the brief layover in Subic the ship's supply officer asked Winthrop's assistance in collecting and inventorying Mayer's personal property for shipping to his next of kin.

"You're Mayer's division officer," he said. "The duty falls on you.

"You have to complete this inventory form and return it and his stuff to me. I'll give the form to the chaplain. He's in contact with the CACO. I'll take care of the shipping"

"CACO?"

"Casualty Assistance Control Officer."

"Oh yeah." Winthrop's mind jumped to a picture of a naval officer and two sailors in dress uniform arriving at Mrs. Mayer's residence carrying the terrible news. A sunny day perhaps, or a rainy day, wouldn't matter; no accurate words existed to describe the shock a loved one must endure upon seeing a US Navy vehicle pull up and disgorge officials in front of one's house. The method of delivery was terrible but swift and undeniable. An unfeeling telegram, a phone call, would not do. For this, a personal visit in full uniform was profoundly appropriate and final.

Many dangerous, grinding, and dirty jobs existed in the Navy, but only intense devotion to duty could help a man perform the CACO duty and then to follow up with assistance in making the final arrangements for the deceased, and to repeat the same function day after day.

And Mrs. Mayer, he thought of her.

Winthrop enlisted Bode's help. Together they retrieved Mayer's uniforms and meager personal stuff from his locker—a few pairs of civilian pants, a couple of shirts and the rest uniforms, underwear, and socks, all Navy issue, and his wallet. They retrieved his copy of "The Bluejacket's Manual," a correspondence course for third-class, a *Playboy* magazine, and a few pornographic pictures from Taiwan. They trashed the magazine and tore up the pictures which they refrained from listing on the form. The whole business took a half-hour.

Unfortunate, such a brief time to wrap up a man's service.

Bode took Mayer's address so he could write to his mother. Winthrop figured the chaplain would draft a letter for the captain's signature and knowing Mayer only slightly, decided not to write to her himself.

Wish I could ask Mary about this. Should I write anyway?

In the end he never resolved the question and failed to write.

34

After the standard R&R in Olongapo with friendly bartenders and willing girls, a satiated crew threw off all lines and steamed for home on August 5, *We Gotta Get Outta this Place* by The Animals blasting out of four track tapes all over the ship.

The long cruise wasn't devoid of work for the crew, but did put a lighter load on all. Spirts picked up. Winthrop's predicted cookout on the after boat deck somewhere in the mid-Pacific mingled in fellowship the crew, officers and enlisted. In the early evening, Boatswain's mate first-class, first division leading petty officer, and product of the Detroit ghetto, Jerome NMI Johnson, tossed his straight-edge razor overboard.

The long tranquil days at sea gave Chief Samuel Early Nobel, hero of the night *Eldorado* fought off the VC, time to make new pals in the CPO mess and establish his new position as LT Trucker's technical assistant for the deck department.

The flagship reached her standard pit stop in Pearl Harbor after 17 days at sea. The crew received notice the chief of naval operations had recommended them for the Navy MUC, the Meritorious Unit Commendation, for their service in the combat zone. Some of the crew flew in their wives and took leave then and there. On Aug 19, *Eldorado* steamed for San Diego.

A local television station interviewed the captain by radio when the ship was a day out of port. His voice shaky with emotion, Captain Ridgway said, "We're coming home."

Some men in the drafting shop got hold of a thirty-foot piece of canvas. They painted it with a reclining *Pogo* alligator holding a cigar and lettering that proclaimed: "How Sweet It Is." They hung the banner on the port side as the flagship entered the harbor.

The *San Diego Union* ran a front-page story about *Eldorado*'s return.

As the tugs pushed her to the pier, a Navy band played. Loved ones who lived in the area, and some who flew in, waved and cheered as she tied up. She had logged 37,140 miles at sea and coordinated twelve amphibious assaults. She was home.

~

As was the case for many crewmen, no relative greeted Winthrop. Guys who completed their service went home to their towns and cities in the heartland and took their places as citizens. No hometown bands or parades greeted them. The public was too embroiled in condemning the war itself to give a damn about them or their service. It was to be years before the politically correct crowd of the time condescended to say, "Thank you for your service."

The early elation at completing honorable service to their country succumbed to despair for far too many veterans. Their contribution went unrecognized or got ridiculed.

~

Captain Ridgeway moved to a prestigious assignment in the Pentagon. At the change-of-command ceremony the new commanding officer announced the posthumous awards of the Purple Heart and Silver Star to Seaman Mayer. He called Chief Nobel front and center to receive a bronze star medal. Winthrop, Larsen, and the watch standers of that night in Da Nang Harbor received letters of commendation.

Winthrop reflected on these events while flying home to Syracuse to recover his car. He planned to drive from his folk's house to

244

Ohio where he could spend much of his thirty days leave visiting Mary before going on to San Diego. Memories of their times together from only a few months earlier seemed vague, as if they occurred in the distant past.

~

A ship follows a cycle. *Eldorado* spent a year operating out of her home port in San Diego. *Mount Mac* and, in turn, the USS *Estes* carried the load in Vietnam until *Eldorado's* turn had come in August, 1968.

The down cycle is a time for training and personnel transfers. A new group of sailors and officers replaced men either finishing their service or going to new duty stations. The ship went through a shakedown period as the new men forged themselves into a solid crew.

Winthrop's friend Jay Dunston finished his active duty, married his sweetheart, and headed for the Northwest where he had accepted a job with the US Forestry Service. Chief Nobel received orders to the Navy Amphibious Base in Coronado. WO4 "Chips" Beasley retired with 30 years of service and many stories for his grandchildren. LT Joe Trucker received shore duty, and Winthrop got a new boss, a mustang officer with long experience in deck department duties.

Ensign Larsen, promoted to lieutenant junior grade the following June, received his qualification as officer of the deck for independent steaming. He would replace Winthrop as a mainstay OOD on the watch list for the next deployment. Recently promoted lithographers mate third-class Zackery Lee grew to be a key man in the print shop. Boatswain's mate third-class Bode reenlisted and took an assignment as leading petty officer on a Swift Boat out of Cam Ranh Bay.

After a year of extensive training, the crew endured the operational readiness inspection, a weeklong series of at-sea drills and

245

exercises to establish the old warship's ability to go back to the Vietnam Theater. This scrutiny established the crew as ready.

A few weeks before the 1968 deployment the ship's operations officer asked Winthrop if he would consider extending his active duty and stay on for the next trip to WESTPAC. Winthrop declined, and a few days later transferred off the ship to the Naval Station San Diego for out-processing.

On June 29, 1968, he showed up at the 32nd Street Naval Station pier in civilian clothes. The Navy band and ship's company family members had gathered there to see the old flagship off once more. A half-dozen sailors from the base arrived serve as line handlers. The command came to single-up and Winthrop stepped forward. The command came down: "Throw off all lines," Winthrop helped toss the bow line from its bollard. That was the last he saw of the ship and crew. Two days later he passed through Barstow, and entered Route 66 with a stop ahead in Ohio and then home.

Epilogue

June 2016

Fred Winthrop stood staring at the rusty hunk of metal, absorbing the sight. Bits of color from the once-proud haze-gray hull flickered through larger patches of oxidization, the only evidence of its life as a warship of a bygone age. Dock cranes, fork lifts, and scrap yard buildings of sheet metal, long past the gleaming stage, blocked much of the view, but he recognized the bones.

The bleak hull, all that remained of the vessel, decommissioned in 1974, now resided in Taipei in a far corner of the ship repair and scrapping yard. The relic served as a floating warehouse for a small firm with limited dockyard space. Like a skeleton no longer supporting a living entity, the remnant offered no solace to Winthrop.

He remembered when the warship's now missing superstructure, a platform for the most advanced electronics of the era, pulsed with sailors. The flag she carried had held sway over amphibious ships in Vietnam. Her obsolete guns, the 5-inch 38, and the two twin-40 millimeter mounts inherited from World War II gave her a proper title as a warship. Her boilers powered her and her generators hummed as the officers and sailors who operated all the machinery of the great ship made her live. They provided the soul of the USS *Eldorado* AGC-11.

You found it. Now, let's go home. Time to visit the kid's grave.

A kid, Winthrop thought, a kid nearly fifty years ago, forever stuck in 1967, the sailor who died on Winthrop's watch.

~

Winthrop picked up a copy of the *New York Times* at the airport in Taipei. He read it idly on the flight to Los Angeles and then LaGuardia. An article on the third page, below the fold, caught his eye, "Normandy Remains Found." According to the article a storm had revealed bones of an American soldier who fell on the first day of the invasion of France.

~

A morning drizzle wet the verdant grass. To Winthrop every blade, every tiny stone, and each drop of water stood out as if echoing the solemn finality of life. He approached across a gentle hill and down a slope toward a grove of trees where the sailor lay, interred for all time.

Winthrop remembered driving through Barstow years before, leaving the Navy to become a civilian. He had pictured himself becoming a success, making big money. It wasn't that simple.

The thoughts and dreams of a near collision at sea often rumbled up through his unconscious. He couldn't leave his war experiences behind. He couldn't simply take on the mundane tasks of routine civilian work. Supercilious new bosses explaining at length trivial tasks had made him want to scream out at times, "Don't you fucking know? I conned a flagship in Vietnam!" They wouldn't even know what the conn was.

Then there was Mayer. How could he explain that night?

They wouldn't understand. They would say Winthrop was crazy. He understood that only his resolve to bury Vietnam and not allow it to bust out in incoherent rage kept him in the sane world. Many veterans could not contain the rage. The attitude of the press forever looking for a crazy veteran to report about added to their distress. Stories and rumors of atrocities in the war circulated and were embellished by the antiwar crowd.

248

Flagship

What kept him in control was the memory of those Marines. If they could move back to civilian life, he could too. Many grunts succumbed to the rage. He would emulate those who handled it. Eventually the raising of a family, moderate success, and the passage of time overcame the demons of the past. Yet his mind often traveled back to those nine months in 1967, the events softened in the recall. Now the flag at the entrance to the Wilmington cemetery brought the same memories rushing back, stark, vivid.

A mound of fresh earth next to Seaman Mayer's simple tombstone marked a new arrival. Fresh-cut lilies next to the sturdy monument proclaimed a recent burial.

He stood before them.

He recalled Seaman Mayer's story that his father helped build *Eldorado*.

No one knew how the elder had fallen. Speculation held that a German pillbox had occupied a nearby site. Perhaps he died from its guns. His decapitated body suggested a violent death. Perhaps he died charging the damn thing, a hero. No one knew for sure, just that he fell on the beach on D-day. As to his son, Winthrop and Capt. Ridgeway alone knew how he fell.

Both stones were government issue. The elder's gave his name and the name of his war, World War II; the son's gave the sailor's name and the name of his war, Vietnam.

The two dead men knew the answer Winthrop sought and couldn't have. The two men knew *why*. And they would know the answer for eternity.

249

Winthrop reached into his pocket, retrieved a 1967 quarter, and placed the memento on the tombstone of Seaman Earnest Royal Mayer. He turned abruptly and started toward the rental car where Mary waited.

As he walked, the slanted rays from the rising sun lit the grassy hillock, making the drying grass shimmer blue-green like the open sea. He heard it then.

A sob.

He turned his head sharply toward the sound.

Nothing.

Another sob.

He stopped.

The tears came then.

ACKNOWLEDGEMENTS AND NOTES

Thank you to my wife Melinda who provided abundant insight and support to me as I wrote this book. I met her in San Diego when I served in the Navy and we have been together ever since.

The men and women of the Sparrowhawk Read and Critique Professional Writers' Group merit special mention here. Audrea, Chavah, George, John, Jonnie, Ken, Lola, Rivkah, Sally, Sandra, Susan and Syd offered fine suggestions.

The sailors I served with on *Eldorado,* provided great inspiration and motivation for my writing. Some of these men are now Facebook friends. I appreciate their encouragement. They are too numerous to mention here without running the risk of overlooking some, but I recall many from my *Eldorado* days.

All of the named amphibious operations mentioned in this book took place on the dates mentioned and the narration of *Eldorado*'s movements rigorously follows the actual record. Although Fred Winthrop and Harley Larsen are fictitious, aspects of the author are found in both. The interpersonal drama of other characters like Johnson, Mayer, and Nobel are fiction. Except for the scene when VC sappers attack, most action events actually occurred.

A.J. Converse
2017

47225225R00142

Made in the USA
San Bernardino, CA
25 March 2017